BUCKS COUNTY
REPORT

Also By Stuart James

Frisco Flat
Judge Not My Sins

BUCKS COUNTY REPORT

STUART JAMES

CUTTING EDGE

ISBN-13: 978-1-952138-77-5

Published by
Cutting Edge Books
PO Box 8212
Calabasas, CA 91372
www.cuttingedgebooks.com

For Richard Wormser and Judy with
gratitude and affection

Whenever a book is written about Bucks County, and there are many, the residents take it apart with glee, attempting to recognize their neighbors. I hate to spoil the fun, but all the characters in this book are fictitious, created from whole cloth from my own febrile mind. I write about a certain area of Bucks County only because I lived there and I like to describe physical locations I know. This story could have been placed in any small town. Essentially, it is a long lecture on morality and love and the various aberrations distorting human emotion. That, at least, is what I like to think it is.

S. J.

CHAPTER ONE

A truck passed on Bradley Road, the sound fading away as it crested the hill and dropped down into the valley. Then there was only the sputter and laboring chug of the power mower to break the morning silence.

Sylvia Thompson was standing at the window, idly smoking a cigarette and watching the young man who guided the power mower, when the phone rang. She ignored the ringing, keeping her eyes and her mind on the muscular back of the young man. When the mower reached the end of one of the long terraces which dropped down the width of the lawn to the pool beyond, the young man jerked the handle about and sent it on its return trip.

The phone persisted, and Sylvia grimaced. The young man wore a T-shirt stretched over his wide chest, and faded jeans hugged his narrow waist and thick thighs. He had a square, simian face with a tilted, insolent mouth, and a cropped brush of blonde hair.

When the annoyance of the phone became too great and it was apparent that it was going to keep ringing, Sylvia turned from the window, crossed the room with long-legged strides, and lifted the receiver.

"Hello," she said.

"Sylvia? This is Agatha Kelsey."

Damn, Sylvia thought, what does the dried-up old bitch want? "How are you?" she said.

"Fine," the voice said. "How are *you?*"

"Not so good," Sylvia said. "I'm working up a passion for the kid cutting the grass." It amused her to shock Agatha, and it further amused her to have people refuse to believe the truth merely because it was spoken in a matter-of-fact manner.

"Really, Sylvia!" Agatha Kelsey said, forcing a laugh. "The way you talk sometimes."

Sylvia had sat through her share of card games, coffee klatches and cocktail sessions with the women of Walkers Ferry, and she knew that behind the public facade there lurked the minds and morals of a gang of stevedores. "Oh, crap," she said, eager to give something for Agatha to talk about, "what's on your mind?"

"Sylvia," Agatha chanted, getting a breathless note in her voice which meant that she needed help for some Village Association project, "I have the most exciting news."

"Why don't you call the *Register*," Sylvia said. "They could use some news."

Agatha giggled as Sylvia had known she would. "No, I mean, really. Walkers Ferry is going to go down in history."

"The Russians going to blow it up?"

"Be serious," Agatha said. "You heard about Dr. Ira Wilson."

"The sex nut?"

"Sylvia, please, I'm trying to tell you something. Dr. Wilson is including Walkers Ferry in his study."

"Why?"

"Why?" The clipped question had thrown Agatha.

"Yes, why? What can he learn from this dried up bunch of biddies?"

"Sylvia, please, you're making it difficult. The study is called: *Sex in Suburbia—An American Phenomena*. He has picked Walkers Ferry because it is different, an unusual community."

It suddenly dawned on Sylvia that the phone call was not for mere gossip. As President of the Village Association, Agatha had probably been contacted and asked to line up volunteers for the Wilson interviewers.

"Are you going to be interviewed?" Sylvia asked.

"Of course," Agatha said. "It is my feeling that these surveys are important."

"What's so important about telling a bunch of college professors how many orgasms you have a month?"

"You can't be serious," Agatha said. "I mean, really, these surveys have already done so much to bring women out of the Dark Ages. I mean, we've found out about our inhibitions and all that."

"I found out about inhibitions when I was thirteen," Sylvia said. "That's when I gave them up. Wanta hear about it?"

"Oh, Sylvia!" Agatha seemed on the verge of tears, and Sylvia was becoming bored with the game.

"Okay, Agatha," she said, "what do you want me to do?"

"I thought you might be interviewed."

"Anything for Walkers Ferry," Sylvia said. "Half the town talks about my sex life as it is, I might as well become official. When do the snoopers get here?"

"There's a general meeting at the school gymnasium on Friday morning at nine," Agatha said.

"I'll be there," Sylvia said. She held the receiver a few minutes more until Agatha had gushed her thanks and said a few more things about the historical significance of the survey, then she hung up.

The conversation left her with a feeling of annoyance. Why had she agreed? It had been the easiest way to get Agatha off the phone, she reasoned. Walking to the maple coffee table between the two large sofas, she took a cigarette from a crystal box, lit it with the silver table lighter.

She inhaled deeply, blew the smoke out, then rubbed out the cigarette in the ash tray. It left a bad taste in her mouth. She was getting nervous again. She crossed to the liquor cabinet, half-filled a tumbler with brandy. She took a long, deep drink of the brandy.

Sex, she thought, the story of my miserable life.

Three marriages had left her financially independent at twenty-eight. She had married Harry the year she graduated from Bennington. He was thirty-seven and successful and had been glad to make a handsome cash settlement. Then there was Arthur, and that hadn't lasted very long because of that party and Arthur's brother, but the father had parted with some gilt-edged securities. Then there had been Cal, and she never could understand that one, because she really loved Cal. There had been no reason for the succession of delivery men, the several husbands of friends.

That was when she had gone under analysis, after Cal had called her a 'damned nympho' and had blackened her eye, and broken the mailman's jaw. When the psychiatrist joined her on the couch, she quit going. He wasn't very good, and she objected to paying for it. She told Cal about the psychiatrist, and he moved out the same night.

She had stopped trying to understand it, but she did try to control it. The phone call, for instance, had interrupted her thoughts about the boy mowing the lawn, and she was glad. It wouldn't last, she'd have to have someone soon, but she'd hold out as long as possible. And then she could go to New York and just get someone out of a hotel bar.

She gulped the rest of the brandy and refilled her glass. Then she went up the staircase and into her bedroom. She put the glass down, and removed the silk pajamas.

Standing before a full-length mirror, she scowled. There was the cause of her troubles. She was tall, five-feet-eight, and her body was perfectly proportioned. Except for her breasts. That's what gets them all drooling, she thought. Her breasts were immense. Turning to the side, she viewed her chest in profile with a mixture of anger and pride. Despite their size, she had no need for a brassiere, and the breasts jutted, firmly and proudly;

soft-textured mounds swelling out from her body, and peaked by long, dark nipples.

Looking at herself made her think of Harry, and she had to chuckle. "I don't know why I ever married you," he had said. "You didn't marry *me*," she had answered, "you married a pair of breasts! And anybody damn fool enough to marry a pair of breasts deserves all he gets!" That did it. He had stormed out of the room. It was true, though, that was the irritating part.

Taking a drink of the brandy, Sylvia went into the shower. She let the lukewarm water caress her for several minutes, then switched it to cold and gritted her teeth. She came out of the shower chattering, but her body tingled. She drank the rest of the brandy and toweled herself dry. Then she went to her closet and pulled a white peignoir off a hanger, slipped her arms into the full sleeves and knotted the cord at her waist.

The brass knocker on the front door clacked. She swept out of the room and across the hall to the stairs. She stopped and gripped the railing, suddenly dizzy. Wheeooo, she thought, the booze hit me fast. Steadying herself, she went down the stairs. She felt suddenly warm and drowsy from the brandy, and she promised herself not to drink so fast in the future.

She opened the door and the grass cutter was standing there. He grinned at her, then his eyes dropped to her breasts, the peaks visible under the filmy material. His tongue flicked over his lips and he swallowed hard, jerking his eyes away.

"The lawn's all done, Mrs. Thompson," he said.

"You want to be paid, I guess."

"Yes, M'am, I guess so."

"Come in." Sylvia stepped back from the door and he entered, standing just inside the room. She closed the door and walked away from him. She stopped at the sideboard, opening her purse. Her hands were fidgeting, and she felt the warm sensation begin to spread up through her body. She fumbled with the purse.

He was even bigger than he appeared from the window. He looked like a college football player, and now his eyes harbored excitement.

"What's your name?" she asked.

"Sam Stafford."

"You live around here?"

"No, M'am," he said, shifting on his feet and taking a breath to expand his chest. "I live in Dunkerville."

"Have a drink?" she asked.

"No, thanks, I don't drink."

"No vices?"

"I smoke," he said, smiling.

"That's all?"

He grinned, and suddenly he took on the look of confidence, his eyes narrowing just slightly.

"How much is it?" Sylvia asked.

"Four dollars."

She took the money and crossed the room. She handed it to him. He stuffed it into a pocket of the tight jeans, but he did not move.

"Kiss me," Sylvia said.

He kissed her in a clumsy way, then stepped back, gasping. "Whew!" he said.

"You must have hard hands," Sylvia said. She reached out, took his wrist, turned the hand over and ran a finger over his calloused palm. She lifted his hand and slipped it inside the peignoir, rubbing the fingers over her breast. She felt him tremble.

Pulling the cord at her waist, she let the peignoir fall open. He caught his breath at the sight of her. The warm, prickling sensation was tearing at her, and she pulled him to the sofa. Grinding herself against him, she kissed him hard, arousing him.

He pushed her over, his fingers clawing at his belt.

I've got to stop this, she thought as the eager hunger subsided. *Somehow, I've got to stop this!*

CHAPTER TWO

It was 9:43 a.m. on June 12th, a Monday morning when Sam Stafford struggled back to his feet, feeling somehow confused and ill-used by the woman on the sofa, who was now completely bored with him. But it was something for him to talk about all summer.

Harley Wayne, a guard on the bridge over the Delaware River which connected Walkers Ferry on the Pennsylvania side to Ferryville on the New Jersey side, noted that the traffic was heavy for a Monday morning, and predicted a heavy tourist traffic for the summer.

At that precise moment at least a dozen people in Walkers Ferry said, "Nice day, but you never can tell. We might get some more snow," and whoever they said it to answered, "I think we had our share."

The sun slanted down over the village which was snuggled in against the hills rolling up from the riverbank, and shafted fat pillars of light through the tall elms and thick, gnarled oak trees.

Walkers Ferry was quaint. It hadn't meant to be in the beginning, it just got that way. In the beginning it had just been the place where the ferry landed. The stage from Flemington crossed there and had rattled off along the rutted York Road to Philadelphia. There was shad running in the river in those old days, and clusters of fisherman's shacks had lined the river bank, and nets dried in the sun. And there were the quarries a short distance up the river where the stone was hammered out for

Philadelphia's cobbled streets. And there was Hoagland's Mill along the river. And damn little else.

But people built houses. Workers at the Mill. Fishermen who figured to stay and raise families. They built the houses themselves of native stone, solid, thick-walled Colonial houses. They built them wherever it suited them, and just left it up to nature for the roads to get around to passing their front doors.

George Washington came along with his bedraggled Army and camped there before the Battle of Trenton.

In time the ferry was replaced by a covered bridge and Walkers Ferry began to take on the appearance of a town. The automobile came, and paved streets followed. But Walkers Ferry was such a hodge-podge of planless thoroughfares it would have been impossible for the road planners to straighten it out, so they paved the narrow, crooked streets, and Walkers Ferry became quaint.

It still wasn't much of a town. Lying there along the river, with the rolling hills of southeastern Pennsylvania embracing it on every side, it had a beauty of quiet dignity.

Some artists found it in the Twenties. It was a quiet place to paint, it was inexpensive, and the narrow little streets and stone houses made excellent subjects for their canvases. And artists are like mice. Let one in and you're soon overrun. Then came the writers and the photographers. Walkers Ferry began to appear in the national magazines.

Walkers Ferry was just 60 miles from New York City, and when it became fashionable to live in the country, and the new radio industry was burgeoning, and advertising was a new trade, the place to live was Bucks County, and the capitol of Bucks County happened to be Walkers Ferry. Houses valued at six hundred dollars went up to six thousand and up and up.

Farmers sold out to the newcomers at fantastic prices, then moved into town and opened hardware stores, lumber yards, grocery stores; and became carpenters and plumbers and stonemasons, to supply and rebuild the houses they had sold.

Chet Parker's father had become a contractor and Chet worked for him as a carpenter, and he was now working on the house in which he had been born. He was in the basement where his mother had stored the home-canned vegetables, and where he had first learned the taste of a cigarette. But now it was a "family room" and Chet was nailing white perforated celotex on the ceiling.

A playwright had first bought the house from Chet's father, and had started the remodeling. A few failures and he went off to Hollywood, selling the house to a radio actor with a yen for young men and a need for seclusion. There was more remodeling, but one day the actor's current companion ran off with a burly ballet dancer, and in a show of grief, the actor decreed never to enter the love-nest again. He sold out cheap to an artist who struck it rich and moved to Europe, selling to the current occupants, Brad Pennington, his wife and daughter.

Brad Pennington was copy chief for a major New York advertising agency. He left the house at seven in the morning for the forty minute drive to the Penn Station in Trenton where he caught an express from Philadelphia and got into New York by nine. He arrived home again at seven each night, except some nights, and then he usually stayed in a New York hotel. These nights had been seldom in the beginning, but they became more frequent, and in the past year Brad Pennington had spent more time in New York than he had in Bucks County.

Chet Parker knew this because he had been working on the house for the past three months, and he wondered how Elizabeth Pennington was taking it.

Standing on the stepladder, leaning back to hammer the nails into the square of celotex, Chet wondered what Elizabeth Pennington was doing at that moment. Probably back in bed, he thought. He knew the bedroom. He had been born there. Of course it was different now, but he knew the house. He could imagine her sprawled out in the big bed, her chestnut hair spilling over the white pillow, her long-legged body mounded in gentle rises under the light cover.

Chet had worked for a lot of these newcomers, had known a lot of the wives. The week, for instance, that he had spent building a breezeway for that Sylvia Thompson. Geezus! He stopped hammering at the thought. Now that one was something. Those fantastic breasts on her, and she could go day and night. It had been almost frightening with that female, but the thing that amused him was that he had been getting three-fifty an hour all the time. But of all the women, this Pennington dame was the real stuff. It made him tingle to think about her, and he had to force himself to go back to the hammering.

Upstairs, sitting at the kitchen table with a cup of coffee before her, Elizabeth Pennington stared out through the window, a troubled expression marring the beauty of her face.

The phone call from Agatha Kelsey had started it, or rather it had brought up the fact that she had to do something about Debbie. It had made her start thinking about sex again and male-female relationships, and what was right or wrong, and she had been over and over that all night. This was coupled with her annoyance with herself for agreeing to participate in the damn Wilson interviews. Her response had been automatic, a result of wanting to participate in community activities, feeling that it was her duty to accept chores pushed upon her by Agatha for the Village Association. Now that she had time to consider it, she didn't see where the Wilson Reports had anything to do with the community or herself.

But it had brought up this other thing again, and she didn't know how to handle it. Damn Brad for not being home. But then she couldn't tell him anyway, because she knew he would be unreasonable about the whole thing. But damn him anyway for staying in New York!

She heard footsteps on the stairs and knew that it was Debbie. She was suddenly nervous. Calm yourself, she thought, we'll just talk this thing out and nothing will come of it. But she knew that she had to be careful, because she did not want to alienate her daughter.

"Hi." Debbie came into the kitchen.

"Morning," Elizabeth said. The tension was broken and she felt sure of herself and a bit foolish for her temerity. After all, this was her daughter. They were close, and there were no secrets between them.

Debbie went to the refrigerator and opened the door, and Elizabeth watched her.

"What time did Carl go home last night?" Elizabeth asked.

Debbie turned, slamming the door and bringing the orange juice to the table. She wore white shorts and a gray print blouse. At sixteen her body was almost fully developed, a youthful replica of Elizabeth's womanliness. The young breasts were high and conical, pressing out taut against the fabric of the blouse. Her waist was narrow and the line of her hips was an easy curve. Her stomach was flat and her long legs tapered to delicate ankles and small feet. Her shoulder-length hair had a reddish tint; Elizabeth's was longer and fell down the hollow of her back. Debbie's brown eyes were larger and there was a sprinkling of freckles over the bridge of the small nose. She sat at the table and poured the juice into a glass.

"I don't know," she said to Elizabeth's question. "Why?"

Was there a note of belligerence in her voice? Elizabeth felt that she had to be careful, had to say it right. Then the thought angered her. My God, she reasoned, this is my daughter. Why am I afraid of what she might think? But the fear still nagged. When Debbie was a small child Elizabeth had determined that she would be a friend to the girl as she grew. But lately it had grown more and more difficult.

"It ... it seemed rather late," Elizabeth said.

Debbie shrugged, but said nothing. She turned her gaze to the window and finished the orange juice. She got up from the chair. "Okay if I take the Volkswagen?" she asked. "I told Marilyn I'd come over and swim today."

"I want to talk to you a minute," Elizabeth said.

Debbie had turned to leave the kitchen and now she stopped and faced her Mother, one eyebrow arched inquisitively. "About what?"

"About Carl," Elizabeth said.

Debbie seemed to brace herself defiantly. "If this is a lecture about being too young to be serious with a boy," she said, "you can save the time. I'm not serious."

A sudden anger swept Elizabeth and she said, "After what I saw last night it might be better if you were serious."

Debbie caught her breath. "What!"

"You and Carl," Elizabeth said, now confused. It wasn't the way she wanted the conversation to go.

"Because we were necking on the sofa?"

"I don't like that expression," Elizabeth said. "And it was a lot more than necking."

Debbie's face reddened as the anger rose in her, stilting her voice. "Are you in the habit of spying?"

"I don't have to spy in my own house," Elizabeth said.

"I thought it was my house, too."

"It is." Elizabeth had the feeling that the conversation had gone wrong. "And that is beside the point."

"We didn't do anything wrong," Debbie said.

"Wrong! What do you call wrong? I came to the head of the stairs and you were spread out on the sofa like a cat in heat."

"Talk about expressions!"

"It fits!" Elizabeth was fighting to control her anger. "What must you think of yourself to let a boy touch you like that?"

"Good Lord, Mother, all the girls do it! It's petting. Don't you read? It's supposed to be good for the emotional balance. We don't go all the way."

"You mean just anyone can come along and slip his hand up your dress? How do you do, Miss, nice day, my, don't you feel nice!"

Debbie giggled and it broke the tension between them. "It's not like *that*," Debbie said. "My gosh, Mother, didn't you do anything when you were my age?"

Elizabeth felt herself flush, and for an instant she remembered the Harbison boy and the night they went to the darkened football stadium. She had been frightened, but she knew why he was taking her there, and she wanted it too. But when it had happened, the awful pain, and his terrible joke—had left her with a feeling of loathing. She had been fifteen, and she hadn't done it again until she was in college. But then it had been wonderful, and Hugh Bascomb had been her biology instructor, and—but that was a long time ago, and she brought herself back to the present.

"We used more control," Elizabeth said.

"Didn't you ever wonder what it felt like to have a man touch you there?"

I nearly went crazy thinking about it, Elizabeth thought, but she said, "That can only lead to serious trouble."

"Not if you're careful. You have to know how to make them stop."

"And suppose you don't want them to stop? I tell you, Debbie, I don't want this sort of thing to go on. I'm afraid I'll have to take it up with your father."

Debbie's eyes widened and the spark of fear appeared in their depths. Her voice was small. "You wouldn't," she said.

"Well, if you don't think there's anything wrong with it, I don't see why you'd mind."

"But not Daddy," she said. "He just wouldn't understand."

"Very well," Elizabeth said, feeling that she had managed to surmount the problem, "but it better not happen again."

"Okay," Debbie said, "but don't be surprised if I break out in pimples." She left the kitchen.

Elizabeth sighed deeply as she heard the front door open and close, but she felt nervous, and it was a feeling she knew well. She used to get it when she'd sit in class and Hugh would be explaining the anatomy of the human body. She would want his hands on her, and the surface of her flesh would seem to be hot. It had always been that way with Brad, and sometimes at parties she would whisper in his ear what she was feeling, and he would chuckle and whisper back that she was a sex maniac. But he would always take her right home, and those were the times when it was the best. The discussion with Debbie had left her feeling that way, and it also had a lot to do with Brad, and the way he was always tired lately. And last week when he had her almost screaming, she was so on edge, he hadn't been able to do anything.

Think about something else, she said to herself. Her thoughts turned to the phone call from Agatha Kelsey, and the Wilson interviews. Sex again! Damn it, she thought, can't you think about anything else? Annoyed, she decided to take a cold shower.

Chet Parker heard Debbie leave the house. He stopped hammering and listened until the sound of the Volkswagen faded away.

He ran his tongue over his lips, making up his mind. If there was one thing that Chet felt he knew about, it was women, and he was damn near sure about this one. He was 28, married with three children, and he was reputed to be quite a local stud.

"I must be part animal," he would tell the drinkers at Kelker's Bar, "because I can always tell when a female wants it. It's as though they have a scent."

He had the scent now, but he was nervous. He knew that he was alone in the house with Elizabeth Pennington, and he had that feeling about her. But she wasn't something ordinary. This was a woman with class, real class. If it turned out he was wrong, he could really have his butt in a sling.

When he heard the creak of the stairs, and knew that she was going up, he put down the hammer and climbed off the step ladder. He was big and rangy with a long, heavy-jawed face. He wore tight levies and a white T-shirt because he knew it accentuated the broad muscular chest, the narrow waist and the powerful legs. His virility was his vanity and he liked to show it.

Taking a deep breath, he squared his shoulders and went up the stairs and into the carpeted living room. He stopped and stared at the stairs running to the second floor. He could stop now, go back to work. But he was determined. He went to the stairs and climbed. He reached the landing and turned to the right. His heart was beating harder and his jaw was set. The bedroom door was ajar.

He walked along the hall, the carpet muffling his steps. He smiled and his confidence swelled as he leaned against the door jamb.

Elizabeth Pennington was unaware of his presence. She sat on the stool by her dressing table. Her nightgown was open down the front. He let his eyes run over her. Up the long legs, over the soft swell of her stomach. Her eyes were closed. She held her breasts in her hands and when her fingers pressed, she grimaced with pleasurable pain.

"A man could do that better," Chet said.

Elizabeth gasped with surprise. Her head snapped around, and her wild eyes fixed on him with disbelief. Her hands grasped the filmy nightgown and she pulled it around her. Her stunned surprise turned to anger. "What do you want?"

"Just looking." There was insolence in his voice.

"Well, you've seen enough. Suppose you get back to your work."

"You sure you want me to leave?"

"Are you crazy?" Elizabeth was on her feet. "I think you better get out of that doorway in the next minute, and get the hell downstairs, or I'll call your boss!"

"I sort of had the feeling you could use a good man." He did not move and the smile stayed on his face.

This can't be happening, Elizabeth thought. She had heard about this sort of thing, and she had heard plenty of stories about Chet, but it couldn't be happening to her. But now the burning sensation was even stronger, and she couldn't take her eyes off him.

"You sure are beautiful," Chet said.

"How dare you talk to me like that!"

"It's a fact," he said.

"Get out of here!"

"I never in my life saw a woman who wanted it so bad," he said.

She gritted her teeth and swore to herself. Damn you, Brad, why did you leave me like this? It's your fault. You know I need it. Damn, damn, why aren't you a husband? Her nerves jumped. She wanted hands on her breasts. Hard hands. Anyone's hands, but not her own.

"I could scream," she said.

"But you won't."

The sonofabitch, she thought, he's treating me like some cheap whore. But that's how I feel. Oh my God, I can't stand this.

He pushed away from the door jamb and came into the room. She stiffened, but she did not move and she did not cry out. Her breath was tight in her throat. He stopped a foot from her. His left hand came up and closed over one breast. Her body shuddered, and a soft moan escaped her lips. He moved to encircle her with his arms, but she pulled away.

"I don't want you to kiss me," she said.

He slipped behind her. His arms went around her, his two large hands joining on the swell of her stomach. He pulled her back against him. He ran his hands down, then drew them up slowly until he cupped her hard full breasts, squeezing them between his thumb and finger.

She squirmed, grinding her teeth against the maddening feeling that was surging through her body. "My God," she gasped, "I can't stand it!"

He released her and she moved away from him. She went to the bed, not looking at him. She could hear him removing the T-shirt. She heard his shoes clump on the floor, and she turned to see him pull the jeans off his legs.

Slipping the nightgown from her arms, she crawled onto the high bed. He came to her, lying next to her, running his hands over her until she shook her head.

When it was over he threw himself on his back. "Whew!" he said. "You're really something."

She regained her breathing and turned her head to look at him. He made her want to retch, and she hated him. She swung her legs off the bed, stooped to retrieve her gown, then padded across the rug to the bathroom. She stopped in the doorway and turned.

"You can get out now," she said coldly.

"What?" Chet sat up, surprised.

"You got what you came after," she said, "now get out."

"Are you kidding? You needed that, Baby."

"That's right," she said, evenly. "I needed it. But I'm no baby. I'm 36 years old, and I don't need it now. I'll thank you to get the hell off that bed and then get off this property as soon as you can gather your tools together."

"Are you trying to say you didn't like it?"

"I'm only saying I want you to leave."

"You liked it, though."

"If it helps your ego any," she said, "you have the prowess of a young bull."

He smiled. "When you want it again just..."

She cut him off. "The only reason I would want you near me again is because I couldn't find a com cob." She had to force herself to say that, but it had the effect she desired. His face fell, the smile gone. "Now get out!" She went into the bathroom, and locked the door.

Leaning on the sink, she stared at her face in the mirror. God, she thought, he *was* good. But it wasn't going to happen again. It made her shudder to think of Brad finding out. My God, that would be the end of everything. She would have to think up a reason for changing carpenters. He'd want to know why, because he had hired Chet Parker himself. She felt the pangs of guilt, and this angered her. Damn him, she thought, if he'd stay home and be a husband it would never have happened. He knows how I get.

She sat on the edge of the bathtub and waited, giving Chet sufficient time to get dressed. She'd pick the next carpenter herself, a nice, old man.

CHAPTER THREE

For a town known for its creativity, Walkers Ferry used no imagination whatsoever in the naming of its streets. There is, of course, Main Street. This is the black-topped road that winds along the Pennsylvania bank of the Delaware River running from Easton in the north to the flat sprawl of Levittown in the south. There is a point where the road becomes Main Street. It curls into the channel of neat white houses with porches and rockers and squares of trimmed lawn. It passes through the two blocks of business establishments: the drug store, the bank, the cleaners, Haber's newsstand, the Chevy agency, the Ferry Inn, the Co-op, the Walkers Ferry Playhouse. It passes over the mill-run, passes Mel's Coffee House, disappears around a corner and becomes River Road again.

The street that comes in from Philadelphia is Route 202 until it suddenly becomes Bridge Street and swoops down the hill, past the post-office and the line of tourist shops, and runs into the bridge. Where John Derry's old stone house stands in named Derry Street. The road running along the old Easton Canal, which cuts the town in half, is called Canal Street. Where the artisans used to have their shops, and where tourists now gather to oggle in windows at the most god-awful collection of high-priced bric-a-brac ever seen, is called Mechanic Street. There are others, about a dozen in all.

Walkers Ferry is a small town, population one thousand. This, of course, does not include the residents beyond the town limit, who live in what is known as the Township. In the Township are the homes of the wealthy, the large fieldstone farmhouses where George Washington is reputed to have slept.

Millie Gerhardt, chief reporter and critic for the Walkers Ferry *Register,* once said: "Isn't it curious that nobody seems to realize that Martha was with George all that time. Everybody in the Township is trying to sleep in more houses than George did, and he was probably the last one around here to shack up with his own wife."

While this was not exactly accurate, it was not without more than a grain of truth, and it was a typical Millie Gerhardt comment. And she would know.

Millie was a copywriter in a New York advertising agency when she first came to Walkers Ferry as the weekend guest of an amorous vice-president. Even then she was more than a match for the average male, and she stayed on as the vice-president's wife. When he gave up the ghost, some say in self-defense, Millie gathered up the stocks and bonds, sold the house in the Township at an enormous profit and moved into town, taking an apartment over the post-office.

At 48, she still had the body for a tight sweater and skirt. "Hell," she would say, "I've had so many passes made at me since I passed 46 that I feel like an aging halfback." Her face had become more femininely handsome and appealing with age.

Her mind was as sharp as her wit, and she had the faculty to dissect the community from stem to stern with an x-ray eye. She liked to rail against what she considered phoney and battle for something she believed in. That was why she wrote for the *Register.* And because she was outspoken and usually right, she had few friends. But her one concrete friendship was with Knox Martin, editor of the weekly newspaper.

On this Monday morning she was slouched in the wooden captain's chair facing the padded swivel which held the spare, angular body of Knox Martin. The steel gray of their hair was the only similarity between the two. Millie was fastidious in her dress. She wore a tweed suit and a cashmere sweater, and even her casual slouch could not detract from the tailored appearance. Knox, on the other hand, was as tousled as a school-boy. He had a long, horse-like face with blue, sorrowful eyes. His hair seemed untouched by a comb. His arms were long, sticking out of his shirt, and they had hands on the ends like spades. He wore rumpled khaki trousers and a pair of heavy, worn brogans on his feet. He had once written a good novel which did not sell, and a bad novel which did. He had bought the newspaper outright with the proceeds of the latter, and had thoroughly enjoyed life ever since. He had the intelligence to appreciate Millie, and together they rode herd on the town's conscience.

The advertising salesman who worked on a fifty-dollar draw and commission was making his rounds, and the girl who did the office work and acted as receptionist was off on an errand.

"Sex," Knox Martin was saying as he stuffed tobacco into his over-sized pipe, "should be relegated to its proper place in society."

"And what is that?" Millie asked, raising an eyebrow.

"It should be treated for what it is. A human function. It doesn't deserve all this publicity."

"I don't know," Millie said. "You certainly didn't miss a trick when Chief Marlowe nabbed those two pansies in the back seat of their car that time."

"That was news," Knox said.

"You wrote it for a laugh and it was sex," Millie said.

"But this is different," Knox said. "This is just straight everyday sex, and these people are distorting it out of shape. I'm not saying it isn't important, but it should be treated the same as any other bodily function like, well, eating."

"Three times a day! My God, Martin, you're a damned satyr!"

Millie laughed hard and Knox screwed his long, homely face into a grin.

When Millie stopped laughing she became serious and said, "Kidding aside, I think you're wrong. This sex thing is a problem. There are too many people goofed up over it."

"That's just it!" Knox exclaimed. "People worry about it. They've made it into some sacred rite. They've made their lives dependent on it."

"That's not the point," Millie said. "You talk as though its something to turn on and off. Hell, it's not just a bounce in the hay."

"What is it then?"

"Oh, brother! If I didn't know you, Martin, I'd swear you were angling for a demonstration. But I'll tell you. Sex with a woman can be the basis for her whole existence. It may be wham-bam-thank-you-ma'am with a male, but the female feels the need and the fulfillment of the sex urge in every fibre of her body."

"But what in hell's name can these surveys do about that?"

"Plenty. When a woman feels something this strongly and all her life she's been told its unnatural or abnormal or indecent, she begins to worry. Some of them get so panicky over the idea that they're latent harlots that they become frigid. These surveys at least show them that they're not alone in feeling the way they do."

Knox puffed on his pipe thoughtfully. "Well," he said, "I'll admit that the Kinsey people are damned sincere in what they do, and they probably do some good with their publications. But this Wilson, now, I can't buy."

"Agatha Kelsey ought to hear that."

"I mean it. I think this Wilson is a fraud."

"Poor Agatha."

Knox squinted his eyes and pointed with the stem of his pipe. "Are you going to be interviewed?"

"Me? You must be out of your mind. My sex life is perfectly adjusted."

"I thought you were a widow?"

"You know damn well I'm a widow and that's what I've adjusted to."

"Don't get angry. Just a question." Knox chuckled and leaned back. "Can't you just see the interviewer with Bertha van Eckman." He changed the tone of his voice. " 'Now then, Madam, do you prefer to look at dirty pictures before or after intercourse?' "

"That's not what they call it nowadays," Millie said.

Knox raised his shaggy brows. "I'll have you know we're a family newspaper," he said.

"It's called coitus."

"I'll be damned," Knox said with feigned amazement. "When I was a kid they called it ..."

"Boffing," Millie said.

"Nope," Knox said, grinning, "it was jazzing."

"Different neighborhood," Millie said.

Knox leaned forward and winked. "Say, old girl, since we're on the subject, why don't we just lock the door—"

"And jazz a little?"

"Boff a little."

"You're a dirty old man, Martin."

"It's in the interest of science."

"Says you."

"Says Dr. Wilson."

"Hah! Look, Martin," Millie said, "do you want me to do a story on this thing or not? I got more to do then trade dirty jokes with old men."

"Millie, my girl, I think that this deserves the deft editorial touch of Knox Martin. The sex habits of Walkers Ferry shall be approached by the mature mind."

A blonde teen-aged girl passed the large window facing Main Street. She wore a light sweater accentuating her young pointed breasts, and tight Bermuda shorts. Her legs were long and tanned. Knox turned his head to watch her pass. "I wonder what they feed these kids?" he asked.

"The mature mind!" Millie rose from the chair and took up her leather purse. "I can see you under the window at Town Hall listening to the interviews."

"In the interest of science."

"I hope they catch you." Millie crossed the office floor. "Have fun. Write it nice." She pushed through the door and was gone.

Knox watched her pass the window, the smile still on his face, then he turned back to his desk and his long brow washboarded. He lifted the press releases pertaining to the Wilson Report. He scanned the printed pages, then dropped them and pushed them away. What would he write about Dr. Ira Wilson? He knew what he should write. He should take the press material supplied by Agatha Kelsey and prepare a simple story for page one that Walkers Ferry was to be honored by a group of scientists intent on adding the intimate details of the suburban ladies sex lives to the mass of material being gathered to release American womanhood from historical prejudices and fears. This would be fine, but Knox did not believe it. He was ready to admit that Havelock Ellis had been an honest and dedicated man, and his *Psychology of Sex* made fascinating reading. He also gave credit to the legitimacy of Kraft-Ebbing, and there was no doubt that the Kinsey organization was honestly trying to discover patterns of human behavior in their surveys. But Wilson was a cat of another stripe. For one thing, Wilson got too much publicity, and most of it smacked of clever press agentry. Knox did not feel that the popular magazines were the place to publish scientific findings. Wilson went after the sensational, just like picking on Walkers Ferry for his interviews. The town was known from coast-to-coast as the hub of a cultural center, a hangout for oddballs. He turned to the papers and glanced at the title of the Wilson survey. *Sex In Suburbia—An American Phenomena.* He wondered what circulation-minded magazine editor had picked that title.

Ira Wilson, Knox knew, specialized in the sensational. The Kinsey people were always trying for a true cross-section of people in their interviews. They had developed a secret method of selection. Not Wilson. He came out in the papers asking for subjects, and it was no surprise that he got a pack of exhibitionists eager to give the details of their life in bed. This, Knox felt, was not only without weight scientifically, it was detrimental if the housewife in Des Moines, Iowa, felt that there was something wrong with her after reading that the "average" housewife had affairs with the butcher, the baker, the candlestick maker.

Knox chuckled and rubbed his chin. Well, he thought, maybe the candlestick maker is a little too Freudian.

He was tempted to turn to the typewriter and voice these opinions in an editorial, but he knew that he would not. There was a better way. He would interview Wilson when he arrived, and he would follow the progress of the interviews. If the man was a fraud, and he was certain he was, it would show in a good deep interview.

Turning to the typewriter, he ran a sheet of yellow paper into the machine. He stopped to scratch his head. Between Wilson and these Bermuda shorts, he thought, a virgin over sixteen will soon be an oddity. He hunched his shoulders over the machine and the big hands began to rattle the keys.

In the living room of the stucco house at the end of Kerwin Drive, Cora Masserly stood with her back to the fireplace, her arms folded. A slender woman of average height, she wore a light summer dress. Her face, though not pretty, was attractive, despite the present look of annoyance. Her hair was black and cut close to her head. There was a sharpness to her features which Sam Masserly had taken as a sign of ascetic intellectuality when he was courting her. It had turned out that it was merely an outward sign of her personality.

Cora tapped her foot impatiently, then she crossed the room, went through the dining room and stopped before the open door of the downstairs bathroom. Sam was standing before the mirror, running a razor over his chin.

"It doesn't make sense," Cora said. "You were planning on studying for your Masters this summer at Penn, and all of a sudden you've decided to teach the summer term. It just doesn't make sense. You'll be teaching one course. Two hours a day. It's ridiculous!"

Sam grunted, but did not answer. It was plain that he had made up his mind and had no intention of changing it, and this infuriated Cora. It wasn't like him to defy her this way.

"Why?" she asked.

Sam lowered the razor and turned from the mirror. He had an intent, serious face, made more so by horn-rimmed glasses, a face befitting his position as instructor of English at Barrows College. He lifted his shoulders slightly in a small shrug. "I decided I'd rather teach," he said in his mild voice.

"Just like that." Cora spoke sharply, nodding her head. "Toss the Master's Degree out the window."

"I've got plenty of time to get a Masters," he said.

"And in the meantime I continue to pinch pennies on your instructor's salary." To Cora the Master's Degree meant a job at State College or better. It meant more money, a chance to climb the social ladder. She had planned on it, just as she had planned everything in their five years of marriage and she did not enjoy the note of rebellion.

Sam continued to shave, and to Cora it seemed that he was deliberately trying to ignore her.

"I'll be damned if I know what you see in Barrows College," she said. "You'd be content to stay there forever."

"It's a good school," Sam said.

"It's a dead-end," Cora said. "Teaching the regular session is one thing. It's a job. But I don't figure this summer session at all."

"Well," Sam said, "it's too late now. I'm signed up for it. I can't back out."

"And I don't understand why I wasn't consulted before you signed the contract," Cora said.

When Sam did not answer, her lips froze in a tight, thin line. She turned from the doorway and walked away. The mixture of anger and frustration was great in her, and behind it was a tinge of fear. Sam's sudden fling at independence upset the orderliness of her existence. It was disconcerting.

Cora had no illusions about Sam's talents or aggressiveness. He was complacent and he was mediocre. She had met him at a Writer's Conference. He was there to attend a poetry symposium. He had ambitions to write. Cora was there looking for a husband. She had ambitions too, but it was to be the wife of a college professor. She knew the path to her goal, and the first thing she needed was the potential professor. She was attractive, she had read a great deal of poetry and criticism. When she met Sam, it was obvious that he was attracted. He was the type she could bend to her will, and she lured him with the pretention of deep interest in his writing.

They were married two months later in the small up-state town where Cora's father was a chalk-smeared high school teacher, a position she loathed.

The honeymoon was abhorrent to her, but it taught her the power of her body. Within a month she had tamed Sam's animal instincts, and he came to her only at her bidding. The whole business of sex was revolting to her, but she did delight in using it as a reward when Sam did as he was told.

Standing again in the living room, Cora wondered where she had slipped. There was something wrong. Of course, there was a way to remedy things. It might not be too late.

She crossed the room briskly and climbed the stairs to the second floor. Entering her bedroom—separated from Sam's by a locked door—she drew her dress over her head and dropped it on the bed. She removed her underclothing and stood nude over her dressing table. It was a slight, but lithesome body. Her breasts were small, evenly moulded and firm. She reached for perfume, dabbed her fingertips and rubbed the scent over the breasts. Going to the closet, she brought out a filmy white gown. She slipped it on, then went to her bed and pulled down the covers.

Sitting on the edge of the bed, she fluffed out her hair, then crossed her legs and arranged the folds of the gown to show the white of her thighs. She had to wait for Sam to finish shaving. It annoyed her, but it had been at her insistence that he use the downstairs bathroom.

When she heard him come up the stairs she took a deep breath and wet her lips. As he passed her door she called in a soft voice, "Sam?"

"Uh?" He stopped. He appeared in her doorway and stared at her.

"Are you in a hurry?" she asked, tilting her head and trying the winsome smile that always worked with him.

There was a long moment of silence. Sam's tongue flicked over his lips and he breathed deeply. "Well, as a matter of fact, I am," he said. "You going back to bed? Do you have a headache or something?"

Rebuffed, she was overwhelmed with confusion. It was a little like having the wind knocked out of her. Unable to say anything, she swung her legs onto the bed and fell back against the pillow. Instantly she recovered. She held her arms out. "Come here, Sam," she said, "I want you."

Sam chuckled. "I'll have to admit its an inviting thought," he said, "but I really don't have time." He stepped back from the doorway and went on to his own room.

Cora knotted her fists and bit her lip to suppress the scream of anger that was in her throat. She held her body rigid until she shook. This had never happened before! Swinging off the bed she stalked to the door and slammed it shut. She stood there a moment, seething, then she went back to the bed and sat. She felt foolish. But maybe he really was in a hurry. With his doltish lack of imagination it would be like him to not realize anything. At least he would know she was angry. Let him sweat it out all day. She could act peevish at dinner, and she'd make him come to her in the evening. That would do it.

She waited until she heard him leave the house, then she got up from the bed and dressed again. There were a few errands to do, then she remembered that she had promised to have lunch with Marcia Storm. This annoyed her because she really didn't like Marcia, but the girl seemed so anxious for her company that it was impossible to refuse. She checked her wristwatch. There was plenty of time.

Beverly Merrick stalked into the kitchen. Her face was flushed with anger and she had her hands clenched until the knuckles were white. Her mother sat at the large round maple table at one end of the large Early American room.

Going straight to the table, Beverly gripped the edge. She spoke in a tight, clipped voice. "Mother," she said, "I'm telling you for the last time to keep that man out of my room."

Claire Roberts took a quick breath and looked up with surprise. At first glance she was a startlingly beautiful woman, but on closer scrutiny the eye penetrated the cover of make-up and the forty-six years were visible. The face was a mask, the vanity of the one-time actress. Claire viewed her daughter's anger with a mixture of dismay and fear. She loved this child of her first marriage, but she knew Mike's lusts, and she feared the girl's youth.

"Whatever do you mean, child?" Claire asked.

"Look, Mother," Beverly said, "that wide-eyed innocent look might have looked grand on the screen, but this isn't fiction. If you want to be married to that big idiot, that's your business. But I can't get dressed or undressed without him standing around watching, and I don't like it."

"I'm sure you're exaggerating," Claire said.

Beverly closed her eyes and took a deep breath. She stood away from the table. She opened her eyes. "Mother. Your husband is doing his best to seduce your daughter. Doesn't that mean anything to you?"

"Bev!" Claire lurched to her feet. "I won't have that sort of talk in this house! How dare you suggest such a thing?"

Beverly swung away from the table. She walked to the center of the room and spun about. "Look at me," she said. "I'm not a little girl. I'm twenty years old. I'm a woman."

Claire looked at the fully-developed girl, and her lips trembled. Her breasts jutted against the fabric of the print blouse. The line of her body swept down to the narrow waist, then flared out over her full hips and long legs. It was a sensuous body.

"You never did like Mike," Claire said, attempting to cover the truth that was within her nagging at the small flame of jealousy. "You were hurt when I married him."

"For God's sake, Mother, talk sense. I got over that sort of thing with your third husband. I admit I don't like him, but not for the reasons you think. He's no damn good, that's why I don't like him."

"Bev! I won't have that!"

"All right! Think whatever you like. I ask only one thing. I want him to stay away from me. If he doesn't then I'm going to move into the dorm at school."

"Now, honey." Claire started around the table, but Beverly turned and walked quickly to the door. "Honey, your breakfast."

"I'll eat in town." She opened the door, went out and closed it after her.

Claire was left standing in the middle of the room. She wrung her hands. Why hadn't Beverly taken that trip to Europe like she wanted her to. It would have been so nice, but she had insisted on taking the summer course. It was nice to have her home, of course, nice that she had chosen to attend Barrows

College, which was so close, but now, right now, with Mike—well, it might have been better.

She was afraid. She stared at her hands. No matter how much hand cream you used, the age showed there. Her life had been built on one thing—beauty. As Claire Carlyle she had been Miss Texas. After that it had been the modeling jobs, and the screen test, and the bit parts in films. My God, she thought, how long ago that was. She had everything then. The beauty, the youth. Men were nothing to her then, because there were always so many. Well, she wouldn't say they didn't mean anything. There always had to be a man. God, she would die without a man. And then there were better parts for her, and although she never became a star, she was well known. There were the marriages. Mark Merrick was the first one, and Beverly had been born, and then divorce. And the others. It got worse with the years, but at least she had enough sense not to marry any more actors like Mark. She had the beauty and the youth, and it was enough for the owner of a hotel chain, a corporation lawyer, and an oilman. She was wealthy. But she was also forty-six, and Mike Roberts was thirty-seven. He was a man, God, he was a man. She knew that he had married her for her money, but he gave her what she needed, and she was afraid to lose it.

But she was afraid to lose Beverly, too.

What could she say to Mike?

The phone rang and it startled her. She went to the wall and took the receiver from the cradle.

"Hello? Oh, hello, Agatha." She half-listened to Agatha Kelsey, her thoughts elsewhere. "Of course," she said. "Well, yes, certainly, I'd be glad to. When is it? Friday morning? I'll be there."

CHAPTER FOUR

David Belson stood at the window staring down at Madison Avenue and 52nd St.

Behind him was the voice of Dr. Ira Wilson. It had a metallic ring, and except for the fact that he knew the man, had spent the past two years with him, it might have seemed like a machine spitting out the words, as cold and impersonal as the IBM machines which digested the facts they fed to them.

But David was more concerned with the flow of walkers on the west side of Madison. They seemed to walk slower after the hunched cold winter, seemed to expand outside of themselves, reaching for the warmth of the sun. From the eighteenth floor the mass was without character. Perhaps it is better that way, he thought. He heard his name and turned from the window.

"It's nice that you're with us," Dr. Wilson said.

The others in the room chuckled at the caustic humor, and David cataloged them. Bill Sharmer sitting on the red leather couch, laughing harder than the rest because he was the least secure. Dr. Hugh Bascomb in the leather chair, his legs crossed casually, the pipe between his fingers, the hair receding from the handsome face, not laughing at all because he did not like Wilson, and because he was a good guy. Howard Denby, Public Relations Counsel, a high-placed pimp, in the chair by the boss, the smirk on his face. Rita Talbot, secretary, recorder of sex histories with no known sex history of her own, trim and efficient, polite chuckle. To hell with you, Rita.

This was the inner sanctum of Research Affiliates, the home office of Ira Wilson, Phd. The room was thickly carpeted, the furniture was masculine and expensive. The windows and one wall were draped to the floor. There was a large Modigliani print on one wall, and behind the vast modern curve of Wilson's desk was a map of the United States, decorated with tiny flags.

"As I was saying," Wilson said, "we will move in force on Walkers Ferry on Friday. That will give us the weekend to set things up, and we can start the samplings on Monday morning. I hope to finish up there by the end of the week."

"The editors of *Argus* are beginning to needle me for some copy," Howard Denby said.

"They'll get it in good time," Wilson said. "David, I want you to run down there tomorrow and see how things are shaping up."

"I'm supposed to finish processing the Scarsdale samplings tomorrow," David said.

"Hmmm. Well, go down on Wednesday then. You can arrange for our accommodations and just stay on and wait for us."

"Does Rita have all the stuff on the contacts?" David asked.

"Yes," Wilson said, "she'll give you the complete dope sheet on the operation. Woman named Agatha Kelsey is lining it up. I want this to come off smoothly so that we can get into Cleveland the following week. That will be the wind-up."

David watched and listened to Wilson with an interest that was new to him. The man was like a General in his planning, but he had the look of a religious fanatic. He had a narrow, ascetic face, the eyes close together with permanently knitted brows giving him the look of perpetual intensity. His jaw was long and determined and his mouth was like two parallel lines, the lips bloodless. He sat on the chair with bird-like readiness, the long, bony hands clasped on the desk.

"That should do it," Wilson said. "We're nearing the end of the present campaign, gentlemen. This next encounter should be extremely rewarding. I know we'll all pull our weight, do our best."

That was the end of it. Rita Talbot scurried to the door and opened it. They filed into the outer office where a dozen typists flailed their machines.

David did not return to his own cubicle. He turned to Martin Bascomb. "I got a date for lunch. See you after."

"After Westport I stopped going out to lunch," Bascomb said. "I stay here and secretly analyze the typists."

David smiled and went through the office. His heels echoing down the empty hall. He turned at the end and stopped at the elevators. He pushed the button that lighted the red arrow.

Before the elevator arrived he was joined by two secretaries from the publicity firm with offices on the same floor. David glanced at the girls, eyeing them both with critical appreciation. How much of the contours they exhibited in their light summer dresses was their own he had no way of knowing, but it was good to look at with an air of absent speculation.

For a moment he tried to remember his impressions when he had first come to this building three years ago. He had been used to the small mid-west college town, the atmosphere of the laboratory and classroom, and he had been strangely affected by the New York office, the Madison Avenue approach to science. It had intrigued him then, but that was a long time ago. Now it was just part of the routine. In his dress, the well-cut brown worsted suit, the striped narrow tie, the button-down collar, the square edge of handkerchief showing, he could have been in advertising or public relations. He had fallen in with the style and attitude of the city just as he had framed his life to fit the large salary he received from Dr. Ira Wilson.

The elevator arrived and he followed the two girls inside. It reached the lobby, the door slid open and the people filtered out, each in his own world, mindless of the sudden and momentary proximity to the others in the small cubicle

David hailed a cab. He climbed into the rear and settled back. "Forty-seventh and Sixth," he said. David glanced at his watch. He was a little late, but not much, and Gwen wouldn't mind.

He turned his thoughts to Gwen. He had to relate her to his current feeling of dissatisfaction. It had nothing to do with her, and yet it did. She was a factor in keeping him tied to New York, and it would be ridiculous to think of Gwen being anywhere else. And what did Gwen mean to him really. He had to face that one, and he didn't like it. Are you in love with her? he had to ask himself, and he had to answer, Dammit, I don't know.

"Here, y'are," the driver said.

"Oh." David paid the driver and got out. He walked a block south and turned in at the American Bar.

The customers here were a strange mixture. At the bar were construction workers from the Time-Life building across the street. There were also several photographers from Life, some people from NBC, several models, a few merchants, a writer's agent with the editor of a girly magazine. David spotted Gwen sitting alone in a rear booth. She smiled as he approached, and as always he was dazzled by the piquant magnificence of that smile. He slid into the booth opposite her.

"Hi. Sorry I'm late," he said, then reached across the table and covered her hand with his.

"I'm the only woman who has to play second fiddle to sex," she said.

David laughed lightly. "We were getting the old pep talk," he said.

"I got one too," she said. There was an edge of excitement in her husky voice, and her green eyes sparkled with anticipation, as they always did when she had been holding something to tell him.

"Ah," David said, knowing that she had attended a reading for a forthcoming play that morning, "how did it go?"

"I got the part," she said.

David was suddenly swept up in her excitement. "You're kidding!"

"I'm not! I got it! I read for Baragren and he leaped up and shouted, 'She's it! That's Emily!' Think of it, David, the second lead in a Baragren show."

He squeezed her hand. "I'm happy for you, Gwen." And then his own problem surged to the front of his mind, and he tried to see her new success in relation to his feelings, his misgivings. In a way, it solved things for him, because it forced him to look at their relationship in a clear light. What were they to each other? He had known Gwen for a year. They had met at a dull cocktail party, and she had left with him to get something to eat. They had fascinated each other from the first, and dinner stretched into a long evening of talk, and while they walked through Washington Square Park and passed the statue of Garibaldi about to unsheath his sword, he had said, "They say that when a virgin passes here he gets the sword out. It's never happened yet." She had laughed lightly at the joke, and by the time they reached the large, circular fountain, he had the confidence to stop and turn her shoulders until she faced him, and kiss her. She returned the kiss, and they went to bed at his apartment that same night. It had been a good relationship. She was beautiful and intelligent. The fact that she aspired to the theater had been a bit amusing to him, but now she had made the grade, and there would be no bringing her back.

And David knew that he could never marry a career girl. He had old-fashioned ideas about home life, despite the years of interviews into the sex lives of Wilson's samplings. He knew that he would never marry Gwen now, and the sudden realization saddened him.

"What's wrong?" she asked. "Aren't you really happy for me?"

"I am," he said. "It's just that I have to leave again tomorrow and I'd rather not." It was easier to lie. In fact, he was glad of the assignment. He wanted time to think about things on his own.

Gwen pouted. "Where to this time?"

"Not far," he said. "Bucks County. A town called Walkers Ferry."

"They have a good summer theater there," Gwen said.

"Well, I'm afraid I won't be seeing much theater," David said. "We'll only be there ten days. Then we go to Cleveland."

"Oh, David! By the time you get back we'll be in rehearsal, and then we'll be on the road. I'll never see you!"

"I'll be out front cheering," he said.

The waiter came to the table and interrupted them. They gave their order, and did not pick up the conversation.

It was a strange meal to David. While neither mentioned it, it was obvious to him that this would probably be the end of their affair. He couldn't pin down exactly what had happened, where this knowledge had suddenly been telegraphed between them, but he knew that Gwen was feeling the same thing. She looked at him rather wistfully, but they had fallen into a silence that was almost reverent, as though each was remembering all the moments that would have to be "them" for all time.

More than ever, he was eager to begin the new project, and some of his dissatisfaction had been submerged.

"David?" Gwen's voice brought him out of the reverie.

Glancing up quickly, David faced her smile. "Yes?"

"Where were you?" she asked, her head cocked.

"I'm not sure." He laughed. "I don't know."

"You weren't with me," she said.

"Actually I was," he said. "I was thinking about us, thinking about ... well ... all the things we've been to each other."

"The summing up," she said.

He nodded. "I suppose that's it. I have a feeling that—"

"Don't say it, David," Gwen said. "I know what you're feeling, but I don't want to hear it in words. As long as it's just a thought I can keep it in the back of my mind and believe that it's not true. I feel so wonderful about the play and I don't want to think that I'm sacrificing one thing to get another."

"Let's have a drink on that," David said. He signalled the waiter and ordered brandy. When the two glasses arrived, he lifted his drink between his fingers and sighted over the rim. Gwen returned his gaze. "Sköl," David said.

He was about to drink when Gwen said, "Wait, David."

Stayed by the urgency in her voice, his eyes widened, bringing a wide smile to her face. "Sköl is not like saying hello," Gwen said. "The English say, 'cheers,' and drink and it means many things, but sköl is very special." As she spoke there was an element of merriment in her eyes. Her words were chosen with care, giving the explanation an aura of excitement, as though she were about to reveal some deep mystical secret. "I'll show you," she said. "You lift your glass like this." She held the glass at chin level, her two fingers embracing the narrow stem. David followed her direction. "Now then, the man looks deeply into the eyes of the girl. They say nothing. They wait until there is a message, something that tells them both that something wonderful is going to happen." Their eyes held, and David began to lose himself in the cool depth of her gaze. He felt his pulse quicken and there was a strange constriction in his chest. "Now," she said.

"Sköl," David said softly.

"Sköl," she whispered.

They sipped the drink and brought the glasses down to the table. Their eyes still held, then Gwen glanced down at her hands. When she looked up her eyes were glistening with the beginnings of tears. "I don't want to talk anymore, David," she said, her voice on the verge of breaking. "Sit there until I leave."

David did not answer. Gwen rose from the booth. She took her light coat from the hanger and draped it over her arm. Reaching for her purse, she glanced at him quickly, then turned and walked away. David watched her go, knowing that a chapter was walking out of his life.

When she had disappeared through the door, David brought his eyes back to the table. He stared at the glass of brandy. Just one sip. The unfinished drink. He began to raise his glass, looked at it and put it down. The brandy at that moment was symbolic of something. He wasn't certain exactly what, but he knew that it must be left. It was tied in with the single sip, the toast, the parting, something left unfinished, left on the note of longing.

David paid the check, took his coat and left the restaurant. He walked north on Sixth Avenue.

Traffic roared in the street. Cabs, buses, trucks fought for position at the lights, spouting fumes and curses, New York on the rush. The sound was a dull roar, leashed beasts straining to run in circles. Store windows glittered in the sunlight. Pedestrians walked on the treadmill of habit, weaving along the sidewalk, avoiding collision, a detached mob brought together for a few moments to move along as a single, surging entity, a current of humanity joined by chance, separately together, moving north or south with the precise intricacies of a folk dance, and soon to be divided by the separateness of mind and purpose. The street was life, the mindless, cacaphonic polyglot of sound and motion.

Turning east on Fiftieth Street, David walked slowly, his thoughts meshing between Gwen and the new project. Gwen's last act was typical of her. She had a knack for taking the commonplace and adding her particular dash of personality to turn it into a ritual of delight. This was, of course, her natural inclination towards the dramatic, but whatever the motivation it added a spice to life that was continually surprising and exciting. David knew that he was going to miss this quality.

Between them both they seemed to have everything necessary for the complete relationship, but something was missing and David could not put his finger on the elusive key. It was natural that he should seek the fault in himself, because he had come close before, but always there was something lacking when he considered a relationship in terms of that completeness that brings a man and woman together for the tenure of their lives.

The difficulty he had faced in himself was that he was left with the feeling of inadequacy, and with the premonition that he was predestined to the single life. Most confusing was the fact that a relationship began with the best of intentions, but somewhere it soured. Why, David thought, why? You meet a girl, you're excited by her, you have much in common. You talk together, share things. For a time this other person is the axis of your existence, your thoughts and movement circling within the sphere of her being. You make love with her, cojoin in the muscling intimacies of the body, blending aesthetic to reality, exploring the cosmos of sensation and emotion. With Gwen it had all seemed complete, but there was always the nagging doubt that could never be justified. This, to David, was the twilight time of the heart's hunger; the cravings inescapably there, but elusive, beyond reach of the mind.

He paused at Fifth Avenue, waiting for the light to change. There seemed to be more pigeons than usual around St. Patricks, wheeling and turning, swooping over the street, weaving their concentric patterns on the warm air. He turned his head to look at a passing girl, one of the sleek untouchables, model-under-glass women. She walked with precise nylon strides, frostily aloof to the construction stiff catcalls from the protection of high girders and the furtive neck-swivels of the earth-bound gentry. David smiled. He stepped off the curb and moved with the crowd. It was a good day, a pleasant day, Spring in the city with the people walking slower, smiling more, heads high and straight as though emerging from coat collars after the hunched and bundled fast-walks of the winter.

The new project took over his thoughts and he felt a surge of excitement and anticipation.

CHAPTER FIVE

Sylvia Thompson prowled the house with the restless anxiety of a cat.

The morning was gone and there was nothing to look forward to but the afternoon. By that time she hoped to be too drunk to give a damn. She held up the tumbler of brandy, squinted her eye, measuring. She snorted and brought the glass to her lips, tilting her head back.

"Sick," she muttered, "God damn sick bitch!" She passed the large mirror in the dining room and stopped. She looked hard at herself with loathing.

"Taking on the God damn neighborhood kids," she snapped to herself. "Rotten, no good bitch. Sex before breakfast and it never means a damn thing."

Castigating herself with the vilest language she could bring to mind, she turned away from the mirror and crossed to the liquor cabinet. She picked up the brandy bottle. "Christ," she muttered, "'did I drink all that?" She emptied the bottle into her glass, then turned and hurled the bottle across the room. It shattered against the stone fireplace. The action did nothing to release her from the feeling of remorse, and she began to pace again.

"Dammit," she railed, "why do I have to feel this way? Why can't I just take them on and enjoy it? But I never do, never do. When I want them they're wonderful, but it's just something to stop the craving."

She was staggering slightly and she felt dizzy. She stopped by the window and stared down towards the pool. "Good christ, why can't I get drunk enough to pass out! I have to do something. I can't just stay in this house the rest of the summer. Maybe I ought to get married again. If I could find someone to satisfy me. Hell, there isn't any such thing. Even that damn Chet Parker wasn't enough."

It occurred to her that she could use new cabinets in the kitchen. But the reason behind the thought assailed her in her mood of self-punishment, and she spun about and hurled the drink away from her.

A sob caught in her throat. She staggered from the window and flung herself down on one of the couches. Her shoulders shook and the tears ran over her cheeks.

"Why am I like this?" she wailed. "Why? Why did they make me like this? I don't want to be like this! I can't stand it! Cal, Cal, don't leave me! I'm sorry! I won't do it again, I swear I won't!"

Sam Masserly was a different man when he stood before his class. His voice was deep and rich and he spoke with deep passion. He stayed close to the rostrum where he kept his notes, moving a few steps to the right or left, but returning to read something, or merely to clutch the sides of the wooden stand for emphasis.

"Lawrence always wrote with a deep love for his native England," he said, "and it is only with sadness that one contemplates that he is known so widely as a pornographer. In 1913 he wrote—" Sam lowered his head to read, quoting from a letter by D. H. Lawrence. "—I break my heart over England when I read the *New Machiavelli*. And I am so sure that only through a readjustment between men and women, and a making free and healthy of this sex, will she get out of her present atrophy. Oh, Lord, and if I don't 'subdue my art to a metaphysic,' as somebody very beautifully said of Hardy, I do write because I want folk—English folk—to alter, and have more sense.' " Sam looked up again. "This was the motivating factor behind his novel, *Lady Chatterly's Lover*, and—"

He was interrupted by the harsh rasp of the bell ending the class. He removed his glasses, smiling. "We'll continue tomorrow," he said.

Chairs and shoes scuffled, chatter immediately filled the room, breaking the mood he had created. Sam gathered his notes together, taking more time than was necessary. He glanced up and she was still sitting, writing in her notebook as the others moved towards the door. He felt his heartbeat quicken. It was confusing the way she affected him. He deposited the notes in his leather brief-case, snapped it closed. He straightened. She was closing her book and rising from the chair.

Sam started for the door the moment she left the chair. The rest were gone and they reached the door together.

"I'm through now," Beverly Merrick said. "I'm going to drive down to the Crossing Park."

Sam did not trust himself to answer. He nodded, and she passed through the doorway ahead of him. He stepped into the hallway and watched her go away from him, enjoying the shift of her body as she walked, enchanted by the way her hair bounced against the back of her neck. His interest in her gave him a feeling of disquiet that was not quite guilt. It was an old story about college instructors becoming involved with their students, but he felt that this somehow was different.

When she was out of sight, Sam went to the left. He stopped at the office to check for messages, then he left the building. He went to the parking lot and climbed behind the wheel of his old Chevrolet.

Driving out of the lot, he made the turn onto Jericho Road, and took his time, thinking about Beverly as he drove.

He hadn't expected to teach the summer course until she had said that she was going to spend the summer in school, and had asked if he was going to teach. His decision had been made in that moment. He hadn't thought about Cora's reaction until later, and by then he had already signed for the course. The Master's

Degree was Cora's idea. It was a good one, practical as all her ideas were, but her motives did not interest him. Even so, it had surprised him that he had made a decision without consulting her. And then he had enjoyed it.

He wanted to be near Beverly. It was as simple as that. There was nothing and everything between them. He had never held her, never kissed her, and yet there was the intangible attraction between them.

Turning on River Road, he drove south. He passed the fields where com would be growing, passed the strawberry fields, the fields already green with alfalfa, the pastures where herds of Aberdeen-Angus grazed.

At Washington Crossing Park, he slowed down. Making a left turn, he drove closer to the river, parked near the cemetery, and got out of the car.

Was it dangerous to be meeting her here like this? There was always the chance of running into someone from town, and it would certainly start a lot of talk. I don't care, he told himself, I honestly don't give a damn.

She was waiting for him, sitting on the grass by the river, her skirt spread out around her. When she heard him approach she got to her feet. He came across the clipped lawn, his steps soundless. There was something different about her, an urgency which communicated to him. She seemed to be waiting for each footfall, and he was conscious of every step that closed the gap between them. It was electric, this knowledge that leaped between them. He stopped several feet from her. Their eyes held and they did not speak. He could not pass the wall that was between them. He was thirty years old, married, her college instructor, and the barrier of convention stilled his feet, throttled his voice.

"Sam!" Her voice was a choked cry. She bridged the gulf, flinging herself towards him, the tears starting in her eyes as she moved.

His arms came up to encircle her as she reached him, and they clung together, mindless of the world about them, feeling only themselves in relation to the other.

Sam held his breath, his heart pounding in his chest, his face burrowed in her hair, savoring the smell of her. He held her tightly, feeling the give of her soft breasts against him, the firm thighs against his. His chest ached and he had to breath.

She lifted her face and tears glistened in her green eyes. She closed her eyes, sighing, and pressed her face into the hollow of his throat.

My God, Sam thought, is it really possible to feel this way?

Cora Masserly parked her 1950 Chevrolet in the lot behind the Ferry Inn. It was not a tourist day and there were only a few cars in the lot.

Slamming the car door and wincing with irritation at the rattle the window made, she walked behind and around the car and entered through the archway into the garden. The tables here were unoccupied. Her heels clacked on the flagstones as she walked to the oak door and pulled it open, releasing the sounds of restaurant. Voices rose and fell, hummed. Glass clinked, plates clattered.

The bartender smiled politely when she entered. The owner, a gray-haired bouncy woman named Mrs. Alston, waved from the kitchen doorway and Cora smiled back.

Five tables were occupied in the somber, wood-paneled room. Marcia Storm was at the end of the bar. Cora went along the bar and stopped next to her.

"I made it," Cora said.

"I'm two up on you," Marcia said. "God, I'm glad to see you. I'm glad to see anybody who hasn't got a runny nose or needs to be changed. I'm especially glad to see *you*." She swung off the bar stool. "Let's sit."

They went to one of the wooden tables and took chairs on opposite sides.

"What's yours?" Marcia asked.

Cora had to consider the price of martinis and lunch. She was careful with money to the point of stinginess, but she suddenly thought of Sam and his new attitude and she thought, the hell with it.

"I'll have a martini," Cora said.

"Two of the same, Nate," Marcia called to the bartender. She settled back and breathed deeply. "Well," she said, "how are you?" And without waiting for a reply, said, "God, you look wonderful. You always look so damn svelte. Me, I always look like I been chasing the hounds without the horse."

Cora smiled, but she had to admit that Marcia did generally look a bit disheveled. Her brown hair was chopped off, not really cut in any stylish way, but chopped, as if she did it herself. Her face was attractive, but it could have been a man's face just as easily. She wore dark slacks and a rough brown sweater, and her only two sure indications of being a female were the lipstick on her lips and the prominent breasts which could not be hidden by the baggy sweater. Her eyes were her most interesting feature and they harbored an intensity which Cora found slightly disquieting. She distinctly did not like Marcia, and she did not quite know what she was doing here, but it was better than sulking around the house.

The martinis arrived. Cora lifted hers and glanced over the rim of the glass. Marcia was staring hard at her, then she smiled. "Here's to birth control," Marcia said.

Cora blushed slightly, and drank a sip of the drink. Marcia's voice was as deep as a bassoon and it carried well.

"I could drink a million of these things," Marcia said. "Christ, after a morning with four kids, I *need* a million."

It was baffling to Cora how Marcia ever managed to have four children. They were all young, all girls, the oldest one was five. She didn't seem to like children, in fact she seemed to detest them. And she seemed to detest her husband, Harvey, just as much. That, at least, was understandable. Harvey was a hulk of a man, the hard, barrel-like, hairy type with the cigar always in his mouth. He looked powerful, like an animal, and Cora could always imagine him in bed with disgust.

"They're beautiful children," Cora said.

"God," Marcia said, "let's not talk about children. Let's talk about doing something after lunch. I'm about nuts."

They ordered another drink, then ate the special of corned beef and cabbage, then drank two brandies, then called for the check which Marcia insisted on paying. "I asked you, baby, remember? This is mine. I gotta make that hairy sonofabitch pay something for all the trouble I seen."

When they left through the garden Marcia walked with Cora to her car. "Why don't we take a drive somewhere?" Marcia asked. "Let's just drive up River Road, maybe stop at the Stagecoach Inn or someplace and have a quiet beer."

"I really shouldn't," Cora said. "Sam will probably be home for lunch."

"Aw," Marcia said, "to hell with Sam for one afternoon. This is our day. Come on, let's drive."

Cora hesitated, but then she thought, it will do him good to sweat it out today, damn good!

They got into the car and Cora backed away from the stone retaining wall. Marcia sat against the door and Cora could feel the intensity of the gaze on her. It made her nervous. She turned the wheel and shifted gears. "God," Marcia said, "you're a wonderful looking thing."

When Beverly stormed out of the house Claire Roberts stood for a long moment staring at the door and chewing her lip. She didn't know what to do. Turning away, she went back to the table and sat down.

Fear nagged at her. She was an attractive woman and she knew it, but she wasn't a girl and she knew that, too. She had to work at keeping the fat off, and nothing could keep the breasts from sagging, and the muscles of the stomach from loosening, and the buttocks from spreading just a bit too much. She needed a man, and she knew that, too, and she didn't need a companion for her old age. She had that man, and she meant to keep him.

Rising from her chair, Claire walked out of the kitchen. She passed through the dining room and into the antique-furnished living room. The stairs were in a corner of the room, the old-fashioned circular type. She climbed the stairs, rehearsing what she would say as she went. She went along the carpeted hallway to the master bedroom. Her husband was in the middle of the floor doing pushups.

He wore only pajama bottoms. He was stretched out, face-down, his body supported on toes and palms. He held himself an inch off the floor, his biceps knotted, the muscles in his back bunched under the strain. He pushed up, snorting, held himself, then lowered his body slowly. His black curly hair fell over his forehead, and sweat glistened on the wide shoulders. He had a juvenile pride in his body, and he exercised daily.

When he completed the push-ups he rolled over on his back, breathing hard. His face was the kind that attracts women. His nose was broken, there was a small scar marring one eyebrow, the chin was heavy, jutting, and the mouth was wide and full-lipped, and could be laughing or cruel. When he sat up he saw Claire and said, "Hi, what's up?"

"Just like to watch," she said.

"Gotta keep it trim," he said, slapping his hard stomach. He got to his feet and started for the shower.

"Mike?"

"Uh?" He stopped and looked back.

"I have to talk to you."

The tone in her voice made him scowl. "About what?"

"About Beverly."

"What's wrong with her?"

"Nothing. Nothing, really, I mean … well, this morning she was … well …"

"She tell you I'm trying to bang her?"

"No! I mean, not really that, but she said … well … damn, I don't know how to say this."

"Just say it. Say it plain." He stood with his legs apart and his hands on his hips. "She said I'm trying to bang her!"

"She didn't! It's just that she said you were always looking at her."

"Well, for Christ's sake, we live in the same damn house! What am I supposed to do, keep my eyes shut?"

"I don't mean that. She said you were in her room."

"I stuck my head in the door to say hello," Mike said. "For Jesus sake, Claire, of course I look at her. She trots around half-naked. What am I supposed to do?"

"I … I don't know."

"You think I need that kid? You think you ain't woman enough for me?" He advanced towards her.

"I don't know. She's so young, so … so …"

"Stacked. So stacked, that it? A kid built like a brick out-house, so I'm supposed to be slobbering after her. Maybe I don't like kids." He took her arms in his large hands and squeezed.

"Oh," she said, "that hurts."

"Maybe I like a woman knows what to do with it, you ever think of that?"

"I think of it."

"I ever let you down?" His fingers untied the cord holding her robe together. "I ever make you think you ain't a woman?" His hands closed over her breasts.

"No, no, Mike."

"You ever get enough of me?" He squeezed her breasts until she ground her teeth with the pain.

49

"No," she gasped, "I never do."

"You want me to show you I ain't after your kid?"

"Mike, you're hurting me."

"You want me to hurt you good? You want me to hurt you the way you like being hurt?" Still grasping her breasts, he propelled her backwards to the bed.

"Yes. I do, I always do."

"You ever get enough of old Mike?"

"Never."

He released her and stripped off the pajama pants with a fast, deft movement. "You want me to tear them things off?"

"No. No, wait." She pulled the robe off her arms, dropped it. She bent over and grasped the hem of the gown and pulled it over her head.

He grabbed her roughly and threw her back onto the bed, pressing her down with his weight. "This what your kid is afraid of?"

"Oh, Mike. Don't talk, don't talk."

"You want it? You want it bad?"

She squirmed and twisted under him. "Yes."

"How bad? How bad you want it?"

"Bad!" Her legs snaked over his flanks and she held him to her.

"You think anybody oughta be afraid of this?" He moved against her, tantalizing her.

"No! No, I'm not afraid!"

"You think that kid oughta be afraid?"

"Oh, Mike, please!"

"Do you?"

"No! No, I don't think she should be afraid."

"You know I'm gonna have her?"

"Mike, please, now!"

"Do you know? Do you know I gotta have that girl?"

"Now, Mike!" She reached down for him with both hands, but he ground close to her and kept her away.

"Do you know that?"

"Yes, yes, I know it! I know it! For God's sake, Mike make love to me! I don't give a damn about her! I don't give a damn! I don't give...a...damn...oh...my God...my God...I don't...don't...oh, Jesus!...Jesus, Mike...Mike!

CHAPTER SIX

It was dusk, and that time of day in Bucks County in the middle of June is a beautiful time.

The sun was gone over Jericho Mountain. The wind was up slightly, but not much, just enough to rustle the trees and bring out the sounds of the cicadas. This was martini time on flagstone patios, get-the-charcoal-out time and start the steaks.

The sloping mounds of hills lay crouched in beginning darkness. Bass leap in the canal, breaking the water. Frogs burp. A speedboat with running lights skims the still surface of the River followed by the frothy trails of a water skier. The single neon sign at the center of town is lighted. It is the slow hour at Haber's newsstand. The lights are on at the Playhouse. There are noisy drinkers in the bar at the Ferry Inn and all over the town are the sounds of supper.

The woman behind the wheel of the station wagon would— to eyes beyond her sphere of life—be envied. She was beautiful. She had the poise that is the special property of the well-bred. She dressed with a natural good taste, and it was obvious that she had the money for the simplicity of cashmere. She lived in a fashionable and expensive section of the country and had no idea or interest in the price of her home. She did not clean her own house, nor was she bothered by laundry or mending. All her problems were promptly attended to with the simple expediency of a telephone call and the signature on a check. Her husband was successful in his business. Her daughter attended an exclusive private school within a mile of their home.

She was typical of the exurban wife. Not burdened by the wealth that could make her a celebrity, but wealthy enough so that she had no knowledge of money.

Her educational background prepared her for a relationship with the arts, and she enjoyed the proximities of intellectualism offered in Bucks County. Her social group included a cross-section of writers, composers and artists. Unlike many of the women in her strata who became addicted to the arts, worshipping the practitioners with a devotion born of their own frustrated desire for expression, she was able to intelligently view the arts with perspective and appreciate her talent for understanding. During college she had shown promise as a poet, but with maturity had come the realization that she did not possess the compulsive neurosis necessary for the full application of her psych in the singleness of purpose. She did not see the goal to which her writing might take her, and not caring to exist in the vacuum of amateurism, she gave up writing. Her talent, she knew, was understanding, and she regarded it as sound and real as the mechanical application in the arts. In many ways her talent was stronger. She was aware, intelligent, emotionally deep, appreciative of the full range of sensory perception. She possessed the vital necessities for writing to a greater degree than many of her successful literary friends, but lacked the knowledge of craft. This craft, she knew, could be learned, but she was content to assuage her curiosity in understanding.

An unusual woman in enviable circumstance driving an expensive, but plain, station wagon over a country road. She did not feel unusual or enviable. She was nervous, frightened; her mind seethed with the imagery of future reality in a fantasia born of guilt and projected against the everpresent backdrop of moral conscience. She was on her way to meet the husband she had betrayed.

Elizabeth Pennington pulled up to the traffic light at the main intersection of the town and stopped. She checked her watch. Plenty of time before the train. She could take it easy down the River Road. The light changed. The Mercury wagon sailed into the turn. She drove onto the bridge and reduced her speed to the 15-mile limit. At the far side the guard nodded to her and she smiled in return. She drove through the three-block business district of Ferryville, turned right at the highway, and upped the speed to fifty.

She was glad that Brad had called to say that he would be home that night, glad to be driving to the station to pick him up. For a moment she had panicked, thinking that he would surely know what had happened in the morning. She had stood looking at herself in the mirror, certain that she looked different, that somehow Chet Parker would have left some stain on her. But she looked the same. She had changed the bed and sprayed the room with scent. Tonight she would have Brad in that bed, and by God, she was going to have him!

Debbie had come home and there was no sign of any argument between them. She hoped that the morning scene had straightened her out. Neither had mentioned it. Everything was all right. Everything was back on the track. Business as usual. Brad would be home and everything would be fine. Never again would there be a Chet Parker. Never! God, how could she have done such a thing?

It was fifteen miles to the Pennsylvania Station. She pulled into the parking lot, then checked her watch. The train wasn't in yet. She shut off the engine, rummaged in her purse for a cigarette.

She was sitting and waiting and smoking when she saw the advance guard of commuters pour out of the station, men and women hurrying, walking with quick purpose. She watched until she saw Brad, then she opened the car door and got out. He stood for a moment looking, then he saw the wagon and started towards it.

What a good-looking man he is, Elizabeth thought. He wore the narrow-lapel lightweight suit with natural ease. He was tall and spare and the new style suited him well. The narrow dark tie was right for the button-down collar of the white shirt. His narrow face right for the short-brim hat. He carried a thin leather attache case and walked with long strides.

He reached the car and Elizabeth had the door open for him on the driver's side.

"Hello, Hon," he said, pecking at her cheek. "How about you drive, huh? I'm beat."

"Glad to," she said. She slid under the wheel and Brad closed the door. Oh, God, she thought, let's hope he's not *too* tired.

Brad opened the door, got in beside her and settled back. He closed his eyes, taking a deep breath, then sat up. He swung the attache case into the back. "Home," he said.

They drove slowly through the city traffic of Trenton, and Brad showed his irritation.

"Tough day?" Elizabeth asked.

"Tough week," Brad answered. "We got a new account, a shoe company. Walker Shoes. Walkers for the walker. You haven't walked until you've walked in a Walker. When a walker is in style."

"Sounds cute," Elizabeth said. She turned down to catch the expressway.

"Only until you've met Walter Walker. A hard, tough bastard with no sense of humor. He wants dignity attached to his product. Refuses to have the word 'walk' in his copy."

"But people walk in shoes."

"He says they don't, and he may be right. He says that Americans move on their asses over a set of wheels. Shoes are a luxury, he says. Oh, hell, screw him, what's been doing?"

"Nothing much. Same old things."

"How's the building coming along?"

"Fine," Elizabeth said. "Fine. But we have to find a new carpenter."

"What's wrong with Parker?"

"We had an argument," Elizabeth said. "I didn't like the way he was doing things. I fired him."

"Jesus, Liz," Brad said, "those guys are hard to find these days. I'll talk to him tomorrow. He'll come back."

Elizabeth started to object, but stopped. She couldn't make too big an issue of it. Maybe later. She'd work it out, but this wasn't the time.

"God," Brad said, pressing his fingers to his temples, "I've got a bastard of a headache."

It had never occurred to Sam Masserly that he was not in love with his wife. It had not occurred to him before this that he had never been in love with anyone. In fact, he really hadn't thought about it very much, and when he did it was merely to excuse love as something created for readers of the *Saturday Evening Post*. Love, he would have said, was a mutual understanding between two people, a plan for getting along together.

Looking across the table at Cora he wondered why in hell's name he had ever married her in the first place. They were eating in the kitchen. The dinner was hastily prepared of frozen foods. They were silent, Cora picking, bird-like, at her food, Sam chewing thoughtfully, wondering.

Here I sit, he thought, in a kitchen eating dinner with a woman I frankly don't give a damn about. The woman there is my wife. She is 29 years old. She thinks sex is something unpleasant that you have to put up with once in awhile to keep a husband in line. She wants me to teach in a bigger college town to give her status. She thinks that I am dull, untalented, easy to handle. She feels that she has married beneath her intellectual level and is therefore a martyr. She thinks children are messy and unnecessary. She hates housework and cooking. She has a sharp tongue and likes to use it like a drill sergeant. She is an unmitigated, god-awful pain in the neck day or night. Then why in hell's name did I ever marry her?

Sam thought back to the time they met. He had wanted to write. Hell, he still wanted to write. He did write in fact, but he would never show anything to Cora. She had been interested then. She had talked writing, writing, writing. In short, he thought, she sold me a bill of goods!

Actually, he had known all these things for several years. But he had merely shrugged and decided that that was the way things went. You got married. You got a job. You learned to live with someone reasonably well. You interested yourself in your work, and to hell with it. That was life!

And now it was as though he had suddenly been led out of the fog and there before him was an exciting land of everlasting sunshine. There was a woman, a young, warm, breathing, human being of a woman, a woman who clung to you, who made your heart hammer and made the blood pulse through your veins, a woman who made you feel young and want to take on the gah-damn world. There was life to grasp, to hold, to savor. There was life to throw yourself into, to wallow in.

He became aware that Cora was speaking to him. He looked across at her. "What?"

"I said I'm sorry I wasn't home this afternoon," Cora said.

Sam took a deep breath. When Cora was sorry about something it meant that she was going to lead him into something or that he was going to be punished for something.

"That's okay," he said, "I wasn't here."

"You weren't? Where were you?"

And now suddenly he realized that he had to lie. It was the first time that he realized that he was an unfaithful husband, and that he was now forced to play a role. He was certain that the lie would be clumsy, and he was nervous. And then he was surprised at his nervousness. If he lost Cora tomorrow he wouldn't miss her a bit. "I had work to do at school," he said. Now why did I lie, he thought, why invent a story?

"Oh," Cora said, satisfied.

It was easy to lie, he thought, and she believed it. I wonder what she would do if I told her the truth, told her that I was with a girl, a young girl, and that I was in love with her. He poked at the fish and smiled.

"What's so funny?"

"Nothing," Sam said, "nothing. Just a story I heard today."

Beverly Merrick was thinking of Sam Masserly. When he touched me, she thought, it was like ... like ... God, there is nothing to describe it. But you can feel it. I felt it, I felt love. Sam, Sam, I love you.

"Penny for your thoughts."

"Wha'?" She looked up and Mike Roberts was smiling at her. He sat at one end of the table, her mother at the other.

"What were you thinking?" Mike asked. "You weren't with your dear old parents."

"Why don't we just get off that parent bit," Beverly said.

"Step-parent," Mike said, smiling. "I am your stepfather."

"The thought makes me ill," Beverly said.

"Beverly!" Claire said. "I don't like that kind of talk."

"Then tell lover-boy to shut up!"

"Really!" Claire said.

"I don't think she likes me," Mike said, grinning.

"Mother, would you mind if I ate in the kitchen?"

"Well ... I ..."

"I'd mind," Mike said.

"I didn't ask you," Beverly said.

"Please," Claire said. "Why can't we just sit and eat like civilized people?"

"Because certain members of the group are not civilized," Beverly said. She pushed back from the table and stood. "Excuse me," she said, "I've suddenly lost my appetite." She turned away from the table and went into the living room, then up the stairs.

Inside her room with the door closing her off from the world she did not like, Beverly put a record on the player, then sprawled on the bed to think.

For the first time in her life she wanted a man, wanted him completely. The depth and ferocity of her feeling frightened her a little. Today, she thought, today on that lawn he could have done anything he wanted to me and I would have helped him. He could have had me on the grass in broad daylight and I wouldn't have cared if there were photographers present.

She was in love. That was the first thought in her mind. She had been attracted to Sam for many months, but today was the first time they had touched. The fact of love was established, and like a woman, she moved on to other facts, cataloging with the reality of a woman. I love Sam, he loves me. Fact. Sam is married. Fact. I must have him for myself. Fact. I don't care how I go about doing it. Fact? Yes, dammit, fact!

There were bound to be complications. Sam hadn't mentioned his wife, but she was there as big as life, and she would have to come up between them sooner or later. What did Sam feel for his wife? Did he ever love her? Why didn't they have children? Could Sam have children? Yes, he must, must! A lot of things were not facts.

She got up to change the record, then paced the room. The important thing was to be near him. That was first. No matter what the complications, she could not stand being away from him. And it had to be more than afternoons in the park.

There was a light knock on the door and Beverly stiffened. "Who is it?" she asked.

"Claire," her mother said from beyond the door.

Beverly opened the door. Her mother came into the bedroom and Beverly closed the door after her.

Assuming that her mother was about to reprimand her for her conduct at dinner, Beverly said, "I'm sorry about the way I acted, Mother, but he baited me. I can't stand that man and he knows it and he baits me everytime."

"I know," Claire said. She went to the window and stood with her back to the room. When she turned her eyes were moist. "I wish I could explain to you what he means to me," she said. She went to a chair and perched on the edge, her hands clasped.

"What do I mean to you?" Beverly asked.

Claire blinked. "You don't know?"

"I'm not sure."

"Haven't I always given you love?"

Beverly was suddenly ashamed of her belligerence "Yes," she said in a small voice. "Yes you have. I'm sorry."

"You said this morning that you might move into a dormitory at school," Claire said.

"I'm sorry, Mother. I was angry."

"That might be a good idea," Claire said.

Beverly stared, wide-eyed. "You mean … you mean you want me to?"

"It's not a matter of what I want." Her eyes were on her hands. "It's just that it might be better."

Beverly was stunned. It had never occurred to her that she might lose out to Mike Roberts. For a moment she was angry and was about to say that leaving would be a pleasure, then she thought: in a dorm she would have hours to keep. She would be confined to the campus. It was going to be difficult enough seeing Sam without the rigors of the college rules. "I'd rather not," she said.

Claire glanced up quickly and there was a note of panic in her eyes. "It would be better," she said. "Better for you."

"Are you ordering me out?"

"Bev!" Claire was on her feet. "Bev, don't say things like that!"

"What am I supposed to say?"

"It's not like that! It's just that with you and Mike in the same house ... well ... I mean, it just doesn't seem to be working out."

Beverly narrowed her eyes. "You wouldn't be afraid of losing your man, would you, Mother?"

Claire caught her breath and her hand flew to her mouth. "How dare you say a thing like that!"

"That's it, isn't it? You're worried about that bastard!"

"Beverly, I won't have this."

"Just keep him away from me, Mother, and you've got nothing to worry about. The very thought of his touching me makes me crawl."

Claire looked confused. She sat down again. "I don't know," she said, "I just don't know."

"He's your husband, Mother, not mine."

"Do you have to be so cruel? I'm only thinking about you."

"Worrying. That's the word, isn't it? Worrying about me, because you know that hairy sonofabitch is a rapist!"

"He's not!"

"Well, whatever he is, tell him to stay away from me. I'm not leaving this house for him or anyone like him. This is my home and I intend staying right here. If he comes within three feet of me I'll kill him. Just tell him that and stop worrying!"

Claire stood. She walked to the door and opened it. "I'm sorry," she said. She went out and closed the door.

Beverly had the urge to call to her, to bring her back and beg her forgiveness. She knew that she had been cruel. But she did nothing. She went to the bed and sat down.

Sam, she said to herself, Sam, I want you, I need you, I have to have you and forget all this ... all this!

Elizabeth Pennington came out of the bathroom wearing a new shortie nightgown that accentuated the full length and curve of her legs. Brad was already in bed.

Elizabeth stopped in the middle of the bedroom. Was Brad asleep? She had been talking to him a few minutes before. She went to the bed quickly.

He was on his side with one arm outflung. He breathed heavily and his mouth was slightly open. Sound asleep.

Going to her side of the bed, Elizabeth pulled the blankets down and climbed in. She pulled the blankets to her neck, then reached up and pressed the button to extinguish the lights. She lay quietly for several minutes, then she turned on her side and moved closer to Brad. She outlined her body against his, put one arm around him. Her mouth was close to his ear.

"Brad," she whispered. There was no answer. "Brad," she said again. She tugged at him.

"Uh? Wha'?"

"Brad, I want to talk to you."

"Talk? What, what?" He came awake. "What's wrong?"

"I want to talk."

"About what?" His voice was irritated.

"Things. Just things. About us."

"Let's talk at breakfast."

"Brad," she whispered, rubbing her hand over his chest, "I want you."

"Baby, I'm tired. I had a rough day. I gotta be up at six to make the train. Be a good girl and go to sleep."

"That's the way it is?"

"Uh? Oh, look, Honey, don't be like that. Honest to God, I got a rough week ahead. I came home tonight to get away from it."

"That's the only reason you came home?"

"Liz, for Christ's sake stop the hurt-wife theatrics. I'm tired. It's as simple as that. What the hell do you expect after all these years of marriage?"

"I expect my husband to make love to me." She was not whispering now, but speaking in a matter-of-fact manner. "I don't expect it every damn night, but I expect him to be man enough and want to enough to make love to me once in awhile. I expect him to come home more often and spend more time with his family."

"You also expect to eat."

"Other wives eat and their husbands come home and they go to bed with them and they make love to them once in awhile!"

"Lower your voice," Brad snapped. "You want Debbie to hear all this nonsense."

"Nonsense? Is that what this is to you?"

"Oh, dammit, Liz...."

"It's not nonsense, Buster. I just asked you to make love to me and you refused. That isn't nonsense."

"Will you keep your voice down?"

"You afraid Debbie will hear about boys and girls? Well, just listen, Captain of the Advertising Industry, your daughter knows more than you'd ever guess!"

"What do you mean by that?"

"If you'd stay home more often and see your daughter you might not have to ask that." She rolled away from him.

Brad was up on one elbow. "What's this about Debbie?"

"Nothing," Elizabeth said wearily. "Forget it, Tycoon. She was petting with a boy and I had to call her down about it."

Brad was silent a moment, then he stretched out flat again. "Damn," he said, "I certainly don't understand women."

"You sure don't, Buster," Elizabeth said to herself, "You sure as hell don't."

CHAPTER SEVEN

It was Wednesday, the sun was shining, and Walkers Ferry wore the day like a resplendent cloak.

David Belson parked the station wagon with the lettering, *Research Affiliates,* on the door. He backed into a parking space by a meter in front of Dr. Cogley's house. He got out, locked the door, then fed the meter a nickel. He turned and crossed the street and entered Haber's newsstand where he expected to find a telephone so that he could call Agatha Kelsey.

Knox Martin came out of the drug store while David was parking. He noted the name on the car and stopped. He watched the young man cross the street, then he followed.

Inside Haber's, David decided to put the call off a moment, and went to the counter. A juke box wailed behind him, but the customers did not seem to notice. Four women sitting on the far side of the counter glanced at him, then resumed their conversation. Two men sat further down from him, and one teen-age boy sat reading a magazine. The young, pretty girl behind the counter came to him and he ordered coffee.

"Make that two coffees, will you, Joanie," Knox Martin said, taking the stool next to David. "You must be with Dr. Ira Wilson."

David showed surprise. "Word travels fast in this town. I just got here."

"I saw you park," Knox said. "I'm the editor of the local paper. Name's Knox Martin."

"I'm David Belson. Your name seems familiar."

"I wrote a book once," Knox said. "It kicks around now and again."

The coffee came and they both went through the ritual of sugar and cream.

"When does the great man arrive?" Knox asked.

"Friday."

"And what do you think of the sex possibilities in our little town?"

David smiled, liking the appearance of Knox Martin and particularly his wry comments.

"I haven't checked your night baseball schedule yet," David said.

"No team."

"Then I'd say we ought to do pretty well."

Martin grinned. "I should say you ought," he said. "Where you be staying?"

"We have reservations at the Ferry Inn. I don't know where it is."

"Just a block down the street," Knox said. "I don't imagine you'll be busy for dinner if you just arrived, so how about if I join you there?"

"I'd like it fine," David said.

"Good. How about six o'clock? I never could get used to this dinner-at-eight business."

"Fine."

Knox finished off his coffee and stood. "See you this evening." He turned to leave and bumped into a girl who was passing him. He recovered, laughing, and took the girl's arm. "Dammit, Athena," he said, "If I was younger I would have done that on purpose."

"You're young enough for me any old time, Mr. Martin," the girl said, smiling.

David turned at the sound of her voice. It was a soft voice with just a bit of huskiness. And the voice belonged to a pretty girl. She was small, but her body was perfectly proportioned to her height. She had blonde hair woven into a single thick braid, worn over one shoulder. Her face was round, the eyes blue, the nose small. The full-lipped mouth was laughing, and there was a slight separation between her two front teeth, which, for some reason, made her even more attractive.

"Athena," Knox said, "I'd like you to meet a new friend of mine. David Belson. Athena Wells."

"Hello," she said and the voice was a caress.

"How do you do," David said.

"Athena is one of my very favorite people," Knox said. "Buy her a coffee and I'll tell you all about her tonight."

"Thanks a *lot*," Athena said.

"It'll all be good," Knox said.

Athena took the stool next to David and Knox left. "You must be new here," she said. "I haven't seen you before." She spoke with the open candor of the small town, a comfortable ease of manner that was strange to one from the city.

"About as new as possible," David said. "I just got here."

"Oh. You know Knox from somewhere else."

"No, I just met him."

"But he said that you were a friend."

"That's funny, but I feel the same way about him. There's something about him."

"It's honesty," she said. "It sticks out all over him. You must have it too or he wouldn't have introduced us."

"Oh?"

"Knox is protective," she said. "I haven't any family and he has sort of adopted me. You made a good impression."

David smiled, but did not answer. He stirred the coffee. The girl disturbed him in a pleasant way. Her candor was disarming and he enjoyed listening to her.

"He's really wonderful," she said, "but he ought to be married."

"Why?"

"Because it's a shame to waste such a good man. He could make the right woman happy."

"That sounds like a typical female cure-all for everything," David said.

She laughed. "I suppose you're right. Maybe Knox would be miserable with a woman around him all the time."

David glanced down at her hand and saw that she did not wear a wedding band. She noticed his appraisal and smiled.

"I'm not married," she said.

"I'm sorry," David said. "Curiosity."

"That's quite all right," she said. "I looked for a wedding ring the moment I sat down. Of course, not all men wear them, and that's not fair."

"Why isn't it?"

"Because a girl is generally looking for a man just as much as the man looks for a woman. Very few of us like the roll of being the other woman, and most of us are so wrapped up in the nesting instinct that we really don't want to disturb someone else's nest."

"Contrary to popular belief."

"Of course," she said, "but the belief was started by men."

"You don't like men?"

"Adore them," she said, "but I can still be just a little bit critical of them."

"You don't spend much time criticizing Knox Martin," David said.

"He likes me," she said. "I'm the one the town talks about. Every small town has a girl they talk about. Knox Martin doesn't, except to stick up for me. He shouldn't really, I guess, because I've certainly given them plenty to talk about."

"What?"

"I was in love."

"That's all?"

"Have you ever been in love?"

"Well, I guess I ... well, I don't know. I mean, I've thought I was in love, but I've never been sure."

"Then you've never been in love. And neither have most people, and that's why they hate to see somebody really in love. It embarrasses them, because they're always hearing about love, and reading about it, but they don't know what it is."

"What is it?"

"The most wonderful slow death on earth."

David smiled. He had interviewed hundreds of women about their sex lives, but he had never once discussed love with any of them.

"This is pretty potent conversation for two people who met three minutes ago," Athena said.

"I was thinking that myself."

"I guess I talk too much," she said.

"You talk good. I like it. What can town gossips say about someone who just happened to fall in love?"

"Plenty. I had the audacity to also have a baby, and before you feel sorry for me, I wanted it, I love it, and I'm awful glad I got it. Knox knows how I feel."

David wasn't quite certain what to say. He had never met anyone quite like this girl. Her honesty was startling. "Isn't it ... I mean ... well, in a small town like this, wasn't it kind of rough?"

"Not really. I was scared to death, of course, but it isn't so bad. I was always disliked because I was pretty, so I was used to that. I was afraid the town might be cruel to the baby, but they're not. If anything, they're just the opposite."

"How old are you?"

"Twenty-two," Athena said.

"Why didn't you marry this man you were in love with?"

"He was married, still is."

"You still in love with him?"

"Little bit, not much. He's been nice about it all. How long will you be in town?"

The speed with which she changed the subject and more or less announced her departure took David back. "A week or two," he said. "I'm with the Wilson interviewing team."

"The sexologist?"

"The same."

"We'll have to have a talk."

"We did."

"I mean a long talk. Where are you staying?"

"The Ferry Inn."

"Wonderful. I work there waiting tables during dinner. Let's have a drink when I get finished."

"I'd love it."

"Me too." She got up. "See you tonight." She gave him the full depth of her smile, then turned and walked to the door.

David watched her go. In ten minutes he had met two people who interested him very much, and he had all but forgotten that he had work to perform. He forced his mind back to business, took out his notebook and looked up the phone number of Agatha Kelsey. He left a half dollar by his cup, got up and went to the phone booth.

Sam Masserly felt the pangs of disappointment when he saw Beverly gather her books at the end of the lecture and leave the room with the rest of the class. His eyes followed her to the door, but she did not turn back or make any sign towards him.

Leaving the room, Sam expected to find her waiting in the hallway, but she was gone. The discovery annoyed and angered him, but he chided himself: Why should she be waiting? What have you got to offer her except a lot of trouble? She's just using her head. You're thirty years old. You're married. You don't make hardly enough to support the wife you've got. For Christ's sake, act your age.

He followed the usual route to the office, checked his box for messages, found nothing. He left the office, walked along the hall to the main entrance.

Suddenly he wasn't interested in teaching the summer term, and it annoyed him that he had made the decision. It further annoyed him to realize that only the girl had prompted him to spend the summer teaching instead of working towards the Master's Degree. He would rather it had been some other motive, something a little higher than merely leching after one of his students.

Leaving the building, he crossed the mall to the parking lot.

Beverly was standing by his car and he had to resist the urge to run.

"I've been waiting for you," she said.

"I'm glad."

They stood facing at the side of his car. It was an awkward moment, each wanting to embrace the other, each resisting the urge, the nervousness growing between them.

"Where can I meet you?" she asked.

"Let me take you. We'll drive."

"No. It wouldn't look right. Just tell me where."

"When you left the room with the others I thought you were walking out of my life."

"Where can I meet you," she persisted.

"I have to be with you," he said. "I have to tell you what it was like to think of losing you."

"Tell me when you can touch me," she said. "Tell me then. I can't stand being this close and not touching you. Just tell me where to meet you."

"At the Tower?"

"Right away." She turned and briskly walked away.

Sam watched her until she got into her car, then he opened his own car door and slid behind the wheel. He followed her out of the parking area, then along Jericho Road, then south on River

Road. She drove fast and he followed her, a sense of urgency growing in him to match the speedometer. They turned off River Road and wound up the curling road of Bowman's Hill. At the top was a parking lot and the stone tower marking the lookout post used by General Washington while he awaited the Battle of Trenton. Beverly parked, and Sam pulled in alongside her. He got out of his car. There were no other cars in the lot. He went to her car and got in beside her. They hesitated a moment, then she slid into his arms and they held each other for a long breathless moment.

They separated, sat apart, but their eyes held, and the eyes were filled with longing and loneliness and pain and love.

"Now I'll tell you," Sam said.

She lifted her hand and pressed her fingers to his lips. "Don't," she said. "Don't. It will only make it more difficult."

They were silent again. Beverly turned away and stared ahead through the windshield. Her hands gripped the steering wheel. "We have to talk," she said, finally. "Yesterday, the day before, it didn't matter. Now it does. I know you love me. You never have to say it. I can see it, I can feel it. I want you to love me, but I'll want more. Not now, not right away. Just now it is wonderful being near you. Tomorrow, the day after, next month, then I'll want more. I'll want you, all of you. I won't want to have you go home to your wife."

"I'm going to divorce my wife," Sam said.

Beverly turned and faced him. "Are you? Have you told her?"

"Well, no," he said. "I just never thought of it before. When I'm ready I'll tell her."

"It's never that simple," Beverly said. "A woman doesn't like to give up a man to another woman. It has nothing to do with him. It is just a matter of pride."

"That doesn't matter. I want you. That's all there is to it. I'll tell her today if you like."

"It can't be up to me, Sam. I won't start on the basis of taking you away from your wife. That is your decision to make. I want you with me only because you want to be there."

"And what do we do in the meantime?"

"I want to be with you in the meantime," she said.

"Then it doesn't make sense. You want to be blameless, and at the same time see a married man. It just stands to reason that I'll be leaving Cora for you."

Beverly slid over and leaned against him. "I know," she said. "It's a curious kind of female logic. I must like to worry things. I really don't care how I'm with you so long as I'm with you, but I also know that love has to have sunshine or it will die. It just won't grow in back alleys, and I don't think you've had much experience with deception."

"None, to be exact," Sam said.

"This could be very hard on you, Sam," she said.

"I don't see how having you could be anything but good," he said.

"Again I can only say that you don't know the extent to which a woman will go to maintain her position."

"But Cora doesn't really want me," Sam said. "There are times when I know that she actually despises me."

"But that doesn't matter, Sam. She will lose face in the town if you leave her for someone else. If she is the kind of woman I think she is, she'll fight for this, just for the sake of her ego."

"I don't know, Bev," Sam said, dropping his head against the back of the seat, "I really don't know."

"We have to work something out," she said.

"Like what?"

"We could go away," she said.

Sam twisted his head to look at her, surprised by the determination in her face, realizing that he actually knew little about her. This, in itself, was startling. Was it necessary to know someone to love them, really, deeply love them? There was the worn adage that you never know anyone until you live with them. You married a woman before you knew her. Was it just a matter of chance that two people found themselves able to sustain a love in the embrace of living? Had he loved Cora in the beginning? No, he didn't think so. With Cora it had been a matter of a bored young man feeling that he might find the riddle of the essence of life answered by marriage. Compared to what he felt for Beverly, the whole business with Cora was ludicrous from start to finish.

"Could we, Sam?" Beverly said.

"Actually it's the only way," he said. "I'm certain of one thing right now. I love you and I want you near me. But I also want this feeling to grow into something greater and stronger, something that will sustain. I want to give it every chance of blossoming." He spoke with his eyes on the ceiling of the car. "What we have now is an attraction. It is strong, but essentially it is a physical longing. It's a sexual attraction. Although I have never made love to you I know that the only thing that keeps us apart is that we have not encountered the time or place and we both feel that it has to be a spontaneous mating. So we have sex holding us together and this is good, but there is also more. I think of it as a growing thing. Sexual attraction can be a basis, the roots. It must be real and solid to create an anchor, but then from the roots must grow the plant, the stalk, and from the stalk—sustained and fed by love—grow the blossoms, the beauty for the world to see. I want this plant to have every chance of a full life, and I believe that staying here in this town might stunt its growth. Hatred might keep out the sun, and even though the roots are solid, the stalk might grow gnarled, the flowers weak and colorless. I must admit that I never thought about this until now, but for some reason I know that I am right. If we are going to have anything we'll have to go away." He stopped speaking. He brought his eyes down to hers. She stared at him for a long moment, then she moved into his arms.

"Oh, Sam, kiss me, I love you so much!"

Elizabeth Pennington did not rise for breakfast. She feigned sleep until she heard Brad leave the house, knowing that Debbie would drive him to the station. She stayed in her room until she heard the wagon pull up before the house again, heard the front door slam, and knew that Debbie was home.

She rose then and went downstairs. She said good morning to Debbie and received a cold silence. They were in the living room and Debbie was standing by the picture window staring out over the terraced lawn.

"What's the matter this morning?" Elizabeth asked.

Debbie turned. "You told me you wouldn't tell Daddy," she said.

"Tell him what?"

"As if you don't know. I just received a one hour lecture on the fallen woman and how she grew. I was embarrassed to death!"

"Oh," Elizabeth said, remembering that she had mentioned the petting incident to Brad. "I didn't think he would say anything."

"I'll bet!"

"Now just a minute, young lady, I'm not going to have you speak to me in that tone of voice. I happen to be your Mother, and I expect some respect from you."

Debbie's anger spilled over. "It never occurs to parents that maybe they have to earn respect!"

"Just what do you mean by that?"

"After what I heard last night, I don't think you ought to ask that! You were practically shouting!"

"Now, see here..."

"What you said to Daddy, well, I don't think you have any room for criticizing how I act with anyone!" She bolted from the room.

"Debbie!"

The kitchen door slammed. As Elizabeth hurried to the kitchen, she heard the sound of the Volkswagen starting. She opened the kitchen door and called, "Debbie!" But the small car was already kicking up the gravel in the drive and roaring off.

Elizabeth stood there watching the car disappear, then she saw the pickup truck turn into the drive and approach the house. She caught her breath and stared with a mixture of disbelief and panic. The truck rolled up and stopped. Chet Parker opened the door and stepped down.

"Howdy," he said, smiling.

"What do you want here?"

"Mister Pennington called the office this morning before he caught his train. Asked me to forgive and forget and come back. I told him there really wasn't anything to forgive. And I wasn't kidding."

"Well, you can just turn right around and go back!"

"You sure that's the way you want it?" He leered.

Elizabeth tried to imagine explaining it to Brad again, and she gave up. "I don't care one way or the other," she said. "Go to work if you like, but stay away from me!"

"Yes, M'am. But in case you—"

Elizabeth cut him off by slamming the kitchen door. She heard his chuckle and it infuriated her. She knew that she could not spend the day in the house with him, so she went to her room to change, planning to drive to Jenkintown to shop.

Cora Masserly was in the kitchen drinking coffee when the doorbell rang. She had expected Sam home for lunch, and when he had called to say that he was spending the afternoon in the library, it had left her with a vague feeling of annoyance.

Rising from her chair, she went through the house and opened the front door.

"Greetings," Marcia Storm said.

"Oh, hello, Marcia."

"Well, invite me in. I escaped again, and I need company."
She held up a paper bag. "I brought along some booze to kill the
pain."

Cora stepped aside and Marcia entered. Cora closed the door
and followed Marcia into the living room.

"Home sweet home," Marcia said. "Where can I find the ice
cubes?"

Cora led the way to the kitchen. She did not want to spend
the afternoon with Marcia, but there didn't seem to be much she
could do about it. What she wanted to do was just sit down and
think about Sam. He had changed and the change bothered her,
in fact it frightened her. He acted as though she did not exist, and
this was a threat to her.

"It's scotch," Marcia said. "How do you like it?"

"With water," Cora said.

They took the drinks into the living room. Marcia dropped
onto the couch and Cora sat in the easy chair.

"Where's Sam?" Marcia asked.

"He had to spend the afternoon working," Cora said.

"Wonderful," Marcia said. She lifted her glass. "Mud," she
said.

They drank and talked for an hour. The conversation was
general and gossipy. Cora was beginning to feel her drinks, and
she yawned. Marcia got up from the couch.

"Stretch out over here," Marcia said. "This is the time of day
to take a load off your feet."

"I'm all right here," Cora said.

"Oh, come on, stretch out. You'll feel better."

Rather than argue, Cora got up and went to the couch. She sat
down, curling her legs under her. Marcia paced the room, glancing at the books and bric-a-brac, then she went to the kitchen and
mixed fresh drinks. When she came back she sat on the couch.

"How come you never had any children?" Marcia asked.

Cora shrugged. "We've never been in the position to have children," she said. It was the stock answer. She would never have said that she didn't want children.

The conversation dragged and they drank and Cora was getting drunk. She did not notice that Marcia had moved closer to her until she felt her arm on her shoulder. She turned to face Marcia, not quite sure what to say. Her senses were dulled. When Marcia ran a hand over her breasts she wasn't certain just why she had done it, then Marcia's face was close, very close, and she was whispering into her ear.

Cora stiffened and got to her feet abruptly. Her voice was thick, but she managed to say clearly, "I think that you had better go."

Marcia regarded her coolly. "You don't like me?" she asked.

"I think that you had better leave," Cora repeated.

"Very well." Marcia got up. She stood a moment, then turned and went to the door. She stopped there and turned back. "I'm in the book if you want to see me," she said.

Cora said nothing. She waited until the door had closed behind Marcia, then she slumped down onto the couch, trembling. How is it possible? A married woman with four children. How is it possible? But she remembered Marcia's words in her ear.

I'll be good to you. I'll be gentle with you. I just want to hold you. You'll like it, you'll see. I just want to love you. Let me love you.

CHAPTER EIGHT

The Ferry Inn is an institution in Walkers Ferry. It was at one time a stop for the Easton Stage, and the stone stables still stand in the rear of the hotel, although they are now garages and storage rooms. Benedict Arnold stayed there for a night when he was fleeing the authorities. It is where any notables visiting Walkers Ferry take a room during their stay, and the actors from the Playhouse spend the summer there.

It is an "L"-shaped building of three stories. It faces Main Street and Ferry Street. The ground floor houses the bar and dining room, the kitchen, the living quarters of Mrs. Alston. The second and third floors house the guests, some permanent, most transients. The accommodations are clean and spacious, but there is no room with a private bath. On each floor are two baths. "It was good enough for George Washington," Mrs. Alston says, "and it was good enough for John Barrymore. If you don't want to share a bath with those two gentlemen, I'd suggest you go to a motel."

The Ferry Inn flourishes. The food is good and the drinks are honest. The walled garden is a place of gaiety on warm summer nights. The bar and inside dining room are wood paneled and decorated with paintings of Revolutionary times. The tables are polished wood. The room is warmly lighted and it is generally graced with considerable laughter and good conversation. This is the watering place for Walkers Ferry, the right place to be seen.

David Belson and Knox Martin had finished dinner and were now drinking sour mash bourbon on the rocks. They sat at a table parallel to the bar. They had talked a lot and had established a mutual liking and respect. In the afternoon David had looked up Knox's books in the local library, and they had discussed his writing. Local topics had been disposed of, and they were now on the subject of Dr. Ira Wilson.

"Fraud is a pretty strong word," David said. "Just because you don't like Wilson's methods is not reason enough to accuse him of fraudulence."

"It's fraud, plain and simple," Knox said. "It is moral thievery."

"I don't get that."

"Well, take our town for instance. You people come in here. You interview women who have some sort of problem with their sex lives. You have methods for getting them to talk about it. For years they may have kept it to themselves. Maybe they're afraid of it, maybe they don't know how to handle the situation or themselves in respect to the problem. You act as a psychiatrist. You as much as put them on the couch and let them bare the problem. To the troubled person this is like opening a nerve to the air. You take down all the facts. You have a case history. Now what? As far as you are concerned, that's all there is to it until those facts are processed by a machine. But what about the victim, the patient? What about the woman who has bared her secret, laid it open for the world to see? Now is the time she needs help, and you people simply pack your bags and head for the next town. Have you ever stopped to think of the number of wrecks you have left in your wake?"

"I never looked at it like that," David said.

"Never?"

"Well, maybe I thought something like that."

"You're too sensitive not to think about it," Knox said. "I think I know you, David, and I'm sure you see some evil in these surveys."

"Not evil," David said. "I'll admit I have certain dissatisfactions with the methods, but it's not evil. The scientist does not effect cures. He examines, he probes. The cures are up to other people. We're scientists."

"The people who invent the thermonuclear bombs take the same stand," Knox said, "but you know damn well that it is merely a rationalization for guilt."

"With your attitude there wouldn't be any research," David said.

"And maybe we'd be better off."

"Now you're rationalizing."

"Yes, I guess I am. But I still think that your boss is a fake. Just take the matter of all his publicity. If he is such a pure scientist, how come he publishes everything in the national magazines instead of in scientific journals?"

"He wants to reach the masses with his information."

"That's a grand thought, but does he take the money from the magazines?"

"Of course," David said. "That's how he finances the surveys."

"That I don't like. A program like this should be financed by a university or a foundation."

"Wilson wants a free hand in what he does. He feels that an organization would inhibit his findings."

"His methods would be a better word," Knox said. "Don't you think that the fact he is being paid by a big circulation magazine dictates his methods? Isn't he deliberately sensational for circulation reasons?"

"I don't know," David said, "I honestly don't know."

Knox took time to rekindle his pipe. David lit a cigarette. The conversation was hitting David too deeply. It brought to the surface much of what he himself had thought about Wilson and his Madison Avenue approach to science. But he had to defend the man's motives, because if Wilson was a fraud then he, David Belson, was also a fraud.

"What did you do before you went with Wilson?" Knox asked.

"Taught biology."

"You didn't like it?"

"Teaching? Yes, I liked it. But it seemed like a rut. I wanted more. I wanted to be doing something more important, something with more purpose."

"You mean you wanted to taste the big time," Knox said. "Now don't get sore. I'm an older man. I've had some desires of my own. There was a time when I wanted to win the Pulitzer Prize. But I settled for less, or I might say I went after more. I found that sailing along on top of the pile you soon forgot to look down. And only looking down can you find the real essence for life. I came here to start a paper, a small paper, and I stayed here for a lot of reasons. One of them is that I see as much life right here, and have a chance to see it closer and better and have more time to try to understand it than I ever had in New York."

"A lot can be said for the big time," David said.

"Not by me," Knox said. "But of course, I'm a small time guy at heart. Let me ask you a question. Were you a good biology teacher?"

"I don't know."

"Did you love it? I mean did you love the idea of having a part in developing other minds?"

"I guess I thought more about developing my own mind."

"Have you done that with Wilson? Have you really had more time to develop your own beliefs? Or are you actually too busy doing the bidding of the great man?"

"How come I'm getting the third degree?" David asked.

"Because I like you," Knox said. "And also because I'm a damned meddler and I like to have the people I like doing the things I think they'd like to be doing."

"I thank you for that. I'll tell you the truth, Knox. I'm not entirely satisfied with what I'm doing, but I'm not against it either. Something about it bugs me, but until I know for myself what it is exactly, I'll go on with it. The premise is healthy and good. Sex is a bugaboo and has been for generations. We presume to prove and convince that it is a natural function and should not be an area of fear."

"Have you ever been in love?" Knox asked.

"That's the second time I've been asked that today," David said.

"I ask that because in your position it is something you should know about. And you should also wonder why these surveys of yours have nothing to do with love. That word never enters into your questions. There must be a reason for that. I don't know what it is, but it is something you ought to be thinking about. It just might make your computing machines blow a gasket."

"I'll think about it," David said.

"Do that," Knox said. "And now I've got to get back to my office. The paper gets delivered tonight and the boys will be coming back with last week's rejects. This has been real enjoyable. Come by the office tomorrow and we'll talk some more." He pushed back his chair and stood.

David got up. He extended his hand and shook with Knox. "I don't know when I've enjoyed talking to anyone more," he said.

"Another thing you might do tomorrow," Knox said. "Take a run out to our college here. Barrows College. It's a pleasant set-up. Small, but active. You might like it here, and I'm sure they could use some good new blood. Matter of fact, I could fix the deal myself. Take a look."

"I'll do that."

Knox Martin crossed the room. He spoke to several people as he left, then disappeared through the doorway into the hall, then the door closed behind him.

Settling back in his chair, David took a sip of his drink, then checked the clock over the bar. It was eight-thirty and he wondered what time Athena Wells finished work. She was working in the garden and he had only seen her briefly in passing, but he had noted that the waitress uniform had failed to subdue the wonderfully exaggerated curves of her small body. He thought to go into the garden and ask her, but decided to simply sit and wait. A waitress came to his table and he ordered another drink.

It had already been a full evening. The talk with Knox Martin had left him moody. There was an awful lot of truth in what Martin had said, and David recalled his feelings of despair when one of the interviewees had committed suicide. That was six months ago, and it had been in Florida. He remembered her name, remembered that he had interviewed her, and he remembered that at the time of the interview he had sensed some root to her problem, had wanted to talk to her more, to help her. But he had kept his silence, had recorded her, let her go. He recalled the words of Cain. *I am not my brother's keeper.* Wrong! Wrong! Just as surely as Cain smote his brother, you failed that woman. You are your brother's keeper, just as everyone is his brother's keeper. To deny this is to deny your existence as a human being. For some time he had wanted to discuss this feeling with Gwen, but had never been able to. In some recess of his mind he knew that when he fully admitted this feeling of guilty inadequacy he would be finished with Dr. Wilson. Instead he kept it to himself, hoping that something would happen to reassure him. It never did.

Athena came to his table a little after nine. She had changed and was again wearing the skin-tight tapered slacks and a harlequin poncho. She sat across from him, bathing him in her smile. "You're a patient man," she said.

"Not unless there's something good to wait for," he said.

"And a gentleman, too. Keep it up, David Belson, I need flattery tonight."

"Facts, M'am, nothing but the facts."

"I feel better already. Let's get out of here and log some walking time."

"I should think you'd have walked enough for a week."

"It's a different kind."

"Suits me. I used to be the athletic type myself."

David signed the check and they left. Athena led the way, and they went along Main street, crossing the bridge over the mill-run, then turned right on Mechanic street. They walked without speaking as though through some prearranged agreement that talk was not necessary.

The night was warm. A light breeze carried flower scent. Clouds scudded across the sky, illumined by the brilliance of a half moon. The street was a short hill. It was narrow and uneven with crazily placed brick sidewalks. They walked along slowly, pausing to look at the displays in the shop windows. An old-fashioned wooden bridge crossed the canal at the top of the hill, and they stopped to lean on the railing and look down on the dark glass surface of the water. Willows bowed over the towpath below them, the delicate, ragged leaf-laden limbs brushing the water.

"This is a place for thinking," David said.

"Peaceful. I love it."

They were silent, both gazing at the water. Athena straightened and moved off. David followed. They went on along the street. The row of shops gave way to houses and TV seen through front windows, and dark shadows of people sitting on porches and the sporadic hum of summer night voices, and the houses gave way to open field. Now it was a country road with dense woods rising on the left, the yellow lights of distant houses, the moon defining the ragged outline of the dark hills. They walked along in the middle of the road, not touching, but close, feeling close, closer still because of the silence and the night.

"Are we going someplace special?"

"Yes," she said.

"Where?" "Someplace. You'll see."

"It's a secret?"

"Yes. My special place."

They walked for half a mile, then Athena stopped. "We go down here," she said. "Just follow close behind me."

David followed her down a narrow path. They crossed a single railroad track, walked along the bed of the railroad, then descended along another path. The weeds were waist high. David heard the sound of falling water. "Here we are," Athena said.

The moonlight glowed on a grassy clearing. They crossed to the edge of a steep bank, and below was a large pool. A creek ran level with the clearing, then tumbled over a waterfall and boiled and danced in the pool below.

"God, what a wonderful place," David said.

"The kids swim here in the daytime," Athena said. "I have it all to myself at night. I come here a lot."

They sat on the grass at the edge of the bank and listened to the musical sound of the falling water. The multitude of night sounds, the myriad million bugs chirping and sawing, joining in one continuous sound.

"Want to swim?" Athena asked.

"I'm a little unprepared," David said.

"Not really. God gave everyone a waterproof skin for a good reason. It's the only way to swim. I'll show my maidenly modesty by moving over there to undress." She got up and moved off into the shadows.

David was still undressing when he heard the splash of her entering the water. He removed his clothing, then scrambled down the bank and dived into the water. It shocked him at first, but his body adjusted and then it was exhilarating. He looked about for her, saw her head, and swam to her.

"Now you know I'm shameless," she said, laughing.

"Nothing of the kind. This is wonderful. I'd forgotten what it was like to swim in the moonlight."

"Now you're young again."

"You think you're kidding. I feel young. I really do. I feel as though I've missed this, but never realized it until now."

She went underwater. He stayed where he was, treading water, waiting for her to come up. When she did not appear he felt a wave of panic touch him. "Athena!"

"I'm back here."

He turned and she was behind him, a few yards away. "For a minute I thought—"

"I wanted to see what you looked like."

He swam to her. "I was a bit startled."

"I know. I'm sorry. I liked what was in your voice though." She kicked her legs up and swam across the pool with easy, even strokes, then she went underwater and came up under him, grasping his legs. He went under and they both came up sputtering and laughing. They swam, ducked, tumbled in the water until they were both breathless, then Athena swam for the shore and he followed.

The water dripped from her as she climbed over the rocks. The moonlight shadowed and highlighted the flawless contours of her body, and David was awed by her child-like grace. He came up after her and they stood together on the grass. She accepted her nudity with a natural innocence that stilled anything that might have been remotely carnal, and as David looked down upon her, his eyes covering the shoulders, her firm, dark-tipped breasts, he saw only the simple beauty of her.

"The air will dry us in a few minutes," she said.

"You know," he said, "it's a strange thing, but I feel as though we've swam here before, as though I've known you a long time."

"I know," she said.

"You know?"

"Yes, I feel the same way. It's like that with two people sometimes. Not often, but sometimes. It's the only way it should be, really. It's just a waste of time to be with someone unless you know, feel that you're supposed to be with him."

"You know an awful lot for a little girl," David said.

"I don't know anything, I just feel things. If I had brains I'd be different, but I don't so I have to just go along with what I feel."

"What do you feel about me?"

"I feel that you're nice, that I'm comfortable with you. We can be silent together and that's important."

"That's all?"

"That all for now."

"I have the feeling I'm going to be in love with you," David said.

"Maybe," she said. "I know that you want to be in love. You want to love someone and I'm here with you and it's comfortable and we've had fun and I bring out a knightly instinct in you. I'm the pretty girl with an illegitimate child."

"That's not very kind," he said.

"Ah, but it is. I want someone to love me. The things I mentioned are just part of the good I see in you. But I want my man to fall in love with me in the daylight. It's not a game with me. It's a day and night affair. And I know that you have the kind of mind that has to weigh things from all angles. You might be in love with me, but it will take time."

"Do you mind if I tell you that you're wrong?"

"Of course not, I want you to. I won't believe it, but I want you to."

"You're wrong. I'm going to be in love with you."

She took a step forward and pressed against him. He encircled her with one arm and tilted her chin back with his hand. He kissed her, the heat surging through him as her lips responded to his and her fingers dug into his back.

When she took her mouth from his she was breathing heavily. "We'd better get dressed," she said, turning out of his embrace. "Then we can talk about falling in love, and you can walk me home, and I'll make you a cup of coffee."

CHAPTER NINE

Folding chairs had been set up in the high school gymnasium facing the stage. The chairs were filled with women, some brought by Agatha Kelsey's efforts, others present in answer to the story in the *Register*.

"...really such an honor," Agatha Kelsey was saying. "I'm sure that there is no need to say..." And she went on at great length to say what there was no need to say.

David Belson stood in the rear. He did not bother to listen to the woman speaking. His eyes strayed over the crowd, and he wondered why they were there. Were they all exhibitionists, as Knox Martin had said? They couldn't all be. Were they all women with problems? Certainly not if they compared to other sampling groups. He had interviewed hundreds of them and there were many women with a good healthy outlook on sex and life in general. But he had to admit that the balance was certainly in the other direction.

He knew that a lot of the women had not come to be interviewed. Many of them were there just because they went to things. They would just as soon attend a hanging or a PTA meeting or a movie on the life cycle of the tsetse fly. Others were there to see the notorious Dr. Wilson in person and hear him speak. Some were there because they thought the proceedings might be a bit racy and they hated to miss even a tinge of smut. A few would be genuinely interested in the scientific purpose of the samplings, and some would be seeking some answer to their problems, and

some would be there for the vicarious thrill of getting their per-
versions into the record.

"...and I might say," Agatha Kelsey said, "that this is an historical moment for Walkers Ferry. It gives me the deepest pleasure to present to you, Dr. Ira Wilson."

Wilson got up from his chair and walked to the rostrum. He
smiled down at the women and for the moment his narrow, cold
face was friendly and warm. "That introduction makes me feel
like a celebrity," he said. There was desultory laughter. They were
at ease. Here was father beaming down at them. They could be
safe with him. He would listen to them. "I am sure that you all
know the nature of my work. I have come here to Walkers Ferry
for a sampling of the sexual attitudes inherent in your female
population in an effort to categorize your community in relationship to the widely divergent communities in the rest of the
country."

David had heard it all before, but he was always fascinated.
Wilson had a studied way of making the women feel that their
sex lives were important to the course of history, that the way
they jumped into bed was going to affect the force of gravity. He
went over the history of the surveys, hammering away at the science angle. After all, this was the age of sputnik and science was
respectable.

"Our methods are revolutionary," Wilson said. "There are
other surveys, of course, and they use all sorts of methods. We at
Research Affiliates have worked out a system which we feel gets
to the heart of the subject, keeps things on the human level, but
also insures anonymity."

Elizabeth Pennington did not have her mind on the lecture.
She was glad to be there, glad to be anywhere but inside her
house where Chet Parker was working. She looked about her at
the assembled women, idly cataloging what they were wearing,

trying to recall some who were familiar, but not known. She looked at Sylvia Thompson, marveling at the girl's beauty, wondering if all the stories about her were true. She noted that Claire Roberts looked tired. No wonder, she thought, with that husband of hers, then she added to herself, sister, you should talk.

Looking up at the figure on the stage, she brought her mind back to what he was saying.

"…indeed, you might well find the experience of discussing the most intimate portions of your life with total strangers a bit difficult. These are your innermost secrets and it is understandable that you should be reluctant to tell the absolute truth. But I can assure you that my three colleagues and myself are not sitting as judges. You must think of us only as statisticians. We will not see you when we talk to you, although you will see us. We have worked out a list of questions. For these questions we seek answers, nothing more. What you tell us is simply part of the record, a portion of the whole."

Elizabeth wondered what she would tell them. Would they want to know about the episode in the football stadium? Would she tell them about that? And the affair in college, would she want to discuss that with this stranger? She was certain that she would leave Chet Parker out of it. He couldn't be important. It was just that she had been in a weird frame of mind and he happened to be there. The whole thing was disgusting and could not possibly have any bearing on her real life.

"I want to impress upon you that while we wish to investigate into your lives it is not our place to advise you. We are here to do nothing but record. We are not doctors, we are not marriage counsellors. We are here on a scientific mission to collect a portion of your lives, and that is all."

Cora Masserly listened attentively, twisting a handkerchief in her hands. She knew that Marcia Storm was in the room, sitting somewhere in the rear. The thought made her nervous. Marcia had not come near her since that afternoon. When was it? Was it only two days ago? It seemed like a month, or as though it never really happened.

In her limited world Cora had heard about women who loved other women, and in Walkers Ferry there were a number of women of whom it was said they were lesbians. She had always wondered about them, specifically wondering what they did to each other, but it was an area of experience that she would never, *could* never bring into conversation. Somehow, she could not reconcile Marcia with this type. After all, the woman was married and she had four children. That she was a lesbian was unthinkable. What then? What?

"When we assemble our records," Dr. Wilson was saying, "we feed our findings into a complex electronic computing machine. They are digested and through a series of parallels we are able to establish certain trends about the sexual habits of a variety of different types of women. When you are talking to our interviewers you must remember that he is not a man, that he is merely the voice to ask the questions and the hand to inscribe the answers. His approach will at all times be completely clinical, and just as you do not feel shame when disrobing your body before your doctor, you should not feel shame when disrobing your mind before us."

What on earth will I tell them, Cora thought, and what can I say to them about Marcia? Is it necessary to talk about her? It wasn't anything sexual. Perhaps it was just the drinking. But she did have her hands all over me, handling me the way Sam used to before I put a stop to it. When she thought about Sam her brow wrinkled. He was certainly acting strange lately. He had left the house in the morning without waking her or having breakfast, and he hadn't shown the least interest in coming to her room with his disgusting proposals as he used to. She brought her attention back to the speaker.

"I think that about explains our mission here," Dr. Wilson said. "We will begin the interviews on Monday morning. On the way in you were all given a card to fill out. Those of you who will be so kind as to help us in our work here, please present the card at the large table in the rear. Be certain to include your telephone numbers and tomorrow you will receive a call telling you the time of your appointment. While some of you may be seeing me again, I will not be seeing you. And so, I thank you very much for listening to me, and I thank you in advance for your assistance in our project."

Cora lifted her hands and joined the applause as Wilson stepped back. She glanced down at the card in her lap, then lifted it. It contained her name, her telephone number and the day she would prefer the interview. She had written "Monday" on the card. She wanted to get it over with, but she was also curious about the interview.

Sylvia Thompson had not been particularly interested in what Dr. Wilson had to say, but sitting watching him, she had become interested in him as a man. She knew that whatever he might say would be prepared in advance and would in essence be meaningless, but she was intrigued with the way he said things. He spoke as though his voice was divorced from his mind or body. He mouthed a series of platitudes, but his eyes covered the assemblage like the eyes of a hawk. There was a fierce dedication that was written in his face, a fanatic quality that belonged to a traveling preacher. And there was a hardness about him. She imagined that if you could see his heart it would be solid granite with the blood merely piped through.

And the thing that Sylvia found most fascinating was her instinctive knowledge that the man had never been with a woman physically. It was something she would never have ventured to explain, but she was certain that this was the truth. There are some things that a woman who is almost completely physical can feel about a man simply by observing his mannerisms, and Sylvia had made this decision about Ira Wilson.

It was a fascinating incongruity. The idea that the man most noted for his knowledge of the sex habits of women had never had intercourse was thoroughly intriguing to her.

Perhaps out of her constant state of boredom, perhaps because of a feeling of dissatisfaction with men, perhaps she was a scientist in her own way; whatever the reason, Sylvia knew that she had encountered something challenging.

David Belson was waiting by the staff car when Ira Wilson scurried out of the door in the rear of the gymnasium. He said what was expected of him. "It was a good talk."

"Tiresome but necessary," Wilson said. "I guess we better get back."

They got into the car, David behind the wheel, Wilson next to him. They drove down the lane past the high school, paused at the highway, then turned left onto the pavement.

"The newspapermen will be waiting at the Inn," David said.

Wilson nodded. He brought the long, bony hands up to press against his closed eyes, then he rubbed the craggy forehead and trailed his hands down over the thin, drawn face and rubbed the prominent chin.

"Well, David," he said, opening his eyes, "a few more weeks and we'll be finished. Another survey complete." He smiled tightly and there was a note of satisfaction in his voice.

"Then the work begins," David said.

"Yes, but the really tough part will be over. Then there is only the pleasure of seeing our field work come together, see all these bits as a greater work, see all the timid jabberings, all the hesitant little half-truths, all the dirty bits of female perversion summed up in facts and figures. There is a purity in the finished product that you don't find in the interviews. The final result is the thing!"

David was remembering the things Knox Martin had said, also recalling his own disquieting thoughts about the true meaning of the interviews, wondering what Wilson would say if the questions were brought to him. He found himself anticipating with relish the questions that Knox would have for the good doctor.

They turned into the parking lot behind the Ferry Inn and David parked the car near the garden entrance. They got out, slamming the doors, and walked around to the front.

"I asked Rita to have the newsmen gather in your room," David said.

"Good. I called Howard and told him to come down," Wilson said. "He should be here."

David had hoped that Wilson would face Knox Martin without the Public Relations man, Howard Denby, present, and he now wondered why Wilson always insisted that Howard be there. If the man was really sincere, why did he need someone to run his interference?

David and Wilson went up the stairs. Rita Talbot was waiting for them on the landing. She was looking nervously efficient.

"The newspapermen are in your room, Doctor," she said in her dry, officious voice.

"Howard here?"

"Yes, Sir. He's with them."

Wilson led the way down the hall with Rita dogging his steps and David bringing up the rear. The door to Wilson's room was ajar and there were voices from within. Wilson swept into the room.

"Good morning, Gentlemen. Hello, Howard, good to see you."

There were five men in the room. They were seated, but they got to their feet when Wilson entered. When David got into the room, Howard was making the introductions.

"Reed Pernock of the *Philadelphia Bulletin,*" he said. "Milton Barnes, the *Trentonian;* Harry Sachs, *Philadelphia Inquirer;* Bill Marris, *Trenton Times;* Knox Martin, the local paper."

"Pleasure to meet you," Wilson said. "Let me get comfortable." He stripped off his jacket and dropped it onto the bed, then he sat down on the edge of the bed, crossed his legs and gripped one knee with both hands. He looked at Knox Martin. "I wondered what ever happened to you," he said. "I read your book, *Tomorrow's Dawn,* while I was in college. It was a fine book. And then you dropped out of sight."

Knox was visibly taken back by the statement and the man's knowledge of his work. The other reporters were obviously impressed. But David had a moment to glance at Howard Denby, saw the relish with which the press agent took the statement, and knew that Howard had done some research on Walkers Ferry and that Wilson had been briefed beforehand.

"Now, then, I suppose you have a few questions," Wilson said. "As you may know I always try to be candid with the press. I fully realize the importance your reports have on the continuance of my work. So, just fire away."

The reporters looked at one another, then Harry Sachs of the *Inquirer,* asked, "Dr. Wilson, could you give a brief summary of your survey to date?"

"It is much too early for that," Wilson said. "The results must be processed."

"Can you give us an indication of trends," Milt Barnes asked.

Wilson smiled. "I seem to get the same questions everywhere we go," he said, "and they're always impossible to answer."

"Well, Dr. Wilson," the reporter from the *Trentonian* said, "You have been on this survey for almost a year, and in that time you have stated that your findings have indicated something revolutionary in regards to the sex habits of the American female. Can you give us a hint what these findings show?"

"I think that I can tell you something," Wilson said. "This is our next to last sampling, and with the results already processed we have come up with something which you might find a bit startling." Wilson paused for a moment to give his words the feeling of portentous decree. The reporters held their pencils poised. "In the past," Wilson went on, "it has always been thought that the sexual desires were more sublimated. In the samplings we have taken thus far, we find indications that this is not true. This is not definite, you realize, but there are indications. The mass of females whom we have interviewed have shown far more aggression than one might have supposed. This is particularly true of married women. It has always been assumed that the woman merely waited for the husband to approach her physically, but our samplings show that in seven out of ten cases, it is the wife who is the instigator of the sex act."

"Is there a reason for this?" one of the men asked.

"It is a matter of interest," Wilson said. "The husband has other things on his mind, business pressure, bills, and so forth. Sex becomes a secondary thing with him."

"Do you mean that women have sex on their minds more than men?"

"That is precisely what I mean," Dr. Wilson said. "With a man it is a physical act of pleasure. With a woman it is a way of life."

The reporters wrote in their notebooks, heads bowed to the page. David saw Wilson glance at Howard Denby and saw Howard wink slightly. Tomorrow's headlines were set. It was certain that the pronouncement made in this hotel room would be on the news wires, and tomorrow would be read in every city and hamlet of America. It was a million dollars worth of publicity for the series in *Argus* magazine, a tantalizing prediction for the sensation-hungry press. In the past months David had listened to Wilson drop hints about this and that to reporters, giving them just enough to make the story interesting, but this was the first time that he had heard Wilson issue a deliberate falsehood.

"If this is the case," Harry Sachs said, "then what about the widely spread idea that the vast majority of women never achieve an orgasm throughout their lives?"

"Pure nonsense," Wilson said. "We have found that women on the average achieve much greater pleasure from the sex act than men, that their sex lives are much happier, and that they often experience not only one orgasm during coitus, but several."

David scowled and looked at Knox. A wry smile played about the mouth of the elderly editor. He knows, David thought, at least he knows. This is all a goddamned lie. David saw that Knox was about to speak, but Howard Denby also saw it. The press agent stepped in front of Knox and cut off the question.

"Well, fellows," Howard Denby said, "let's wrap it up with that. I told you the Doc would give you something to make the city editors sit up and take notice, now, didn't I? That's front page copy, and you're the first to get it. Now, I know you've got deadlines and these boys have got a lot of sex problems to tangle with. Let's go downstairs and the drinks are on me."

It was a clever maneuver, and David knew that Howard had earned his week's salary. The reporters got up to leave. Knox shrugged and got up with them. They shook hands with Wilson, then went through the door and into the hallway, Howard Denby herding them away.

Rita Talbot came into the room. "Dr. Wilson," she said, "Mrs. Kelsey is downstairs. She has the cards."

"Well, take them away from her, Rita. Then begin working on the schedules. Have Bascomb and Sharmer arrived?"

"Only Dr. Bascomb," Rita said. "Mr. Sharmer is still tied up in the City."

"Very well. Have Bascomb start to work with you."

"Yes, Sir." Rita left.

Wilson got up from the bed. He paced to the window, pulled the curtain aside and looked down at the street. "Quaint little town," he said. "We ought to get our share of screwballs here."

"Sir," David said, "I don't understand that statement you made to the press."

Wilson turned slowly and one shaggy eyebrow was cocked. "Don't you?"

"No, Sir, I don't. I don't think we have the facts to back up that opinion."

Wilson pursed his lips and nodded thoughtfully. "Opinion," he said. "Now that is an interesting choice of words. Opinion. You mean by that, I presume, that I made those facts up, took them out of the air."

"I didn't mean to be rude, Sir, I just—"

"You were right," Wilson said, "absolutely right. Not a word of truth, but excellent newspaper copy." Wilson turned back to face the window. "David," he said, "this is a tough, competitive world in which we live, remember that. I have worked with you for three years, watched you, lived with you. You have one fault. You are an idealist, an idealist in a time when ideals won't buy you a cup of coffee. What I told those newspapermen offends your scientific purity. Forget it. It has no bearing on our work. No matter what they print, our work goes on as usual, and the results that come out of the machines will be the truth. By that time the story will be dead, and the newspapers will be happy to see me contradict myself. In the meantime we keep our work in the public eye. The end, David, the end justifies any means."

"But what has a newspaper story got to do with the 'end?' "

"What do you think our 'end' is, David?"

"What? Why, to complete the survey," David said.

"No, David, that is only part of it. The important thing is to continue our work. To do this we need money, the money, incidentally, that pays your salary. This money comes from publications, and the publishers are eager to underwrite our work only so long as our results sell their publications. You may not like these facts of life, David, but they are facts nevertheless. What I said today will help sell magazines." When David did not answer, Wilson turned from the window. "Would you give Bascomb and Rita a hand with the schedule?"

"Yes, Sir," David said. He turned and left the room. There was much realistic truth in what Wilson had said. If you want to dance, you must pay the piper.

He walked along the hallway and turned into the stairs, went down slowly. Wilson was no doubt correct, he reasoned, but it left a bad taste. He reached the bottom of the stairs and stopped. Howard Denby was saying goodbye to the last of the newspapermen at the front door. The screen closed and Howard turned, a scowl replacing his usual smile.

"Oh, hi," Howard said. "How about a drink? I really need it."

David did not like the public relations man, but at the moment he was curious about him.

"Fine," David said, "I'd like it."

They went into the bar and took chairs at a corner table. Howard leaned back, rubbing his eyes. "This is too early for me," he said. "I had to get the seven o'clock train out of the city." He blinked and yawned. "Brother, what a burg," he said. "I get on the other side of the Holland Tunnel and I might as well be in the Aleutian Islands. The Great American Desert." He lifted his arm and waved his hand in a circle. "There it is," he said. "Land of the Great Unwashed. From the Hudson River to Golden Gate Bridge, the vast intellectual vacuum, stronghold of the *Argus* magazine mentality."

"Some of the best universities are out there," David said.

"Oasis," Howard said. "An occasional watering spot. And besides that there aren't any universities in this country anymore. They're just big high schools. Believe me, when they applied democracy to education they ended learning. Our ideas of mass education had to account for the incredible stupidity of all the buffoons out there, so we just gave up on education. The college student of today has been sold a bill of goods. He goes through those cretin level grammar schools for four years and gets a piece of paper written in Latin that he can't even read and believes that he's a scholar." Howard laughed and slapped a hand on his leg. "Pure public relations, the whole thing. One of the great con jobs of all times."

"You make it sound pretty grim," David said.

"Don't ever think it," Howard said. "I'm just a realist. I can appreciate a con man because I know where I stand with him. You take the Doc. He's got it knocked, because he knows just how stupid the people are. He's selling sex, but he's also got enough sense to play up to the illusion that the Great Unwashed are also scholars."

"You don't think that our work is honest?"

"What's honest got to do with it? What's honest? Wake up, man. The one thing you got to get used to in this racket, or any racket, is wearing the mantle of pure crap. Public relations is just a matter of trying to make the crap smell sweet. They can write books about it and teach it in journalism schools and it still remains crap. Now you take me, I can get up a press kit, write a release, run interference with a bunch of newspaper guys. Any idiot can do that. But I know one thing better than anyone else. I know one thing, and you want to know what this is?" He did not wait for an answer, but winked and said, "I know everybody in the business. I know what everybody drinks. I know what they like and what they hate. I know a little dirt here, a little there. I know who has to get paid off with a jug and who gets paid off with a hooker. I know if they like blondes or brunettes, a leg man from a chest man. That's all I know. Everybody in the business. And believe me, in a tower built of crap you don't find any bricks."

David smiled. "Madison Avenue wouldn't agree with that," he said.

"Agh, honk them," Howard growled. "Look, boy, listen to the old man. This is the big clip-job, the biggest carney on earth. That Madison Avenue, hell, a couple thousand gray-flannel barkers pushing the old shell game. And the midway is all the pre-fab split-levels from Hackensack to Sheboygan. They're all marks, the same country bumpkins who have been crowding the carneys since Barnum went legit. Dress 'em up, give 'em big cars, send the kids to college, and hell, they haven't changed a bit. Sell them hope, give them a look at the future, make their sex lives legitimate, tell them they're gonna get something for nothing and you own them. But don't ever try telling them the truth. Jesus, that would really panic them!"

"I take it you don't like the beautiful common people," David said.

"Like 'em? Me, like 'em?" Howard blinked and his eyes widened. "They make me want to throw up."

"Then how can you stand doing what you do?" David asked. "How do you face each day?"

"What am I supposed to do, drop dead? I gotta eat, and my tastes run to first class fare."

"Do you think Wilson feels this way?"

"Hell, what do I know what Wilson feels. You saw that little act up there this morning. Pure crap and the marks bought it."

"Maybe not," David said. "Knox Martin didn't go for it."

Howard chuckled. "I had to do some fast broken field running around that one," he said. "There's always an exception and he happens to be one of them. But that's just another example of why the con artists will always come out on top. I checked Martin out before I came down here." He grinned. "We really threw him a left hook with the nonsense about his books. He was a threat, but once we had him off balance it was easy. I tell you, boy, the road to success is littered with the bones of sincere guys. Do you think the rest of those newspaper guys gave a damn what we told them? They don't care. They got to get a story in and if we can give them something sensational they're happy. People like Knox Martin don't count. They're always small-time. Hell, let's have that drink and forget it." He turned and signalled the bartender.

David did not say anything. His opinion of Howard Denby was strengthened. Not only did he think that the man was wrong, but he also saw him as typical of the New York success mind. They see the world in the capsule of their own frustrated designs, their minds ingrown to the point where they see the rest of the world in the image of themselves. They had to be wrong! People like Knox Martin and Athena might be in the minority, but the very fact that they existed gave the lie to Howard's conception.

And what about Ira Wilson? Seen from Howard's point-of-view, Wilson was unsavory. David was still undecided, but the wheels of his mind were spinning and facts were clicking into place.

CHAPTER TEN

A gatha Kelsey's parties, according to the hostess, were as democratic as the Fourth of July. A widow of invested wealth, she practiced the new democracy—the belief that anyone who belonged to the Village Association was welcome to her home. Her guest list was the roster of the Association.

If one wanted to spend the evening drinking and talking with the same people they met at the post office that morning, or encountered at the newsstand or hardware store, or rubbed elbows with in the Ferry Inn, they came to one of Agatha's parties. As a general rule the majority ignored her invitations. Even suburbanites can tire of one another, and to be in the same room with Agatha, drinking her whiskey, was an open invitation to serve on the next committee for the Horse Show or Children's Bazaar or one of her dozens of activities. The conspiracy between Agatha and the telephone company was bad enough.

But this Saturday night her guest list was out in force. It wasn't every day that Agatha had a famous sexologist on tap.

The party filled the ground floor of the huge stone house and spilled out onto the flagstone patio where Paul Cortland's Dixie Five tortured the *Muskrat Ramble*. The pool was lighted and several knots of people stood around its edge, but there were no swimmers. Agatha's parties were never that democratic. A buffet lunch covered a long table at the edge of the patio. Two white-jacketed bartenders sweated over the drinks at the portable bar set up in the TV room.

Dr. Ira Wilson was backed up against a bookcase by a pressing group of admirers. Even a studied smile could not dislodge the grimace on his face.

Conversation surged like incoming waves, a rolling mass of words crossing like tides to crash on ears and die out, to be replaced by still more waves, high-low, rising, falling, more words and more words until the overall sound was like the rush of a strong wind. Two hundred people talking and nothing being said.

Exurbia on Saturday night, different from Scarsdale or Westport only in that Bucks County parties seldom have themes; no costumes, no Japanese lanterns, no charades. Everyone present was either part of a couple, the resident half of what used to be a couple before Reno, the adult children of couples. Husbands and wives arrive together, then go their own way. It is considered bad form for couples to stay together at parties. It might be a bit embarrassing, when the booze takes hold, to make a pass at your own wife. There is generally live music at a Bucks County party, but seldom any dancing, unless a few guests stray in from Princeton. The chief sport at a Bucks County party is to stand close to someone's wife, close enough to smell her perfume, close enough to gaze into the valley of her breasts, and talk. The talk might lead to a casual ramble across the lawns and some blurred lipstick, and occasionally a neighbor's wife might be coveted in the bushes, but for the most part it is all talk. There is the usual quota of moral dereliction in Walkers Ferry as in any other healthy suburban community, but not at parties. Parties are for talking, drinking, accidentally nudging breasts to check for resilience, getting someone's wife to pour out the woes of her marriage while you listen sympathetically and arrange to meet her in New York for lunch. An unwritten divorce law—one that is as intractable as tempered steel—in Walkers Ferry decrees that Mother keeps the homestead and Dad shambles off to New York to live in near poverty. This has a heartening effect on the moral discretion of the male.

David Belson and Hugh Bascomb stood together in a corner of the library. They had drinks in their hands. Hugh smoked his ever-present pipe. They watched the changing of the throng around Ira Wilson with interest.

"This is the first time we ever gathered socially with our victims," Hugh said. "I thought it was against the rules."

"I guess Wilson makes up the rules as he goes along," David said.

"You sound a bit chagrined, my lad," Hugh said. "Something bothering you?"

"Oh, nothing much. Idol with feet of clay, that sort of thing."

"Gods must be made of stone to endure," Hugh said. "And even they get tumbled from time to time."

"Guess you're right. I was called a foolish idealist yesterday."

"Munitions makers call pacifists idiots. It's only according to what side you're on who the bigger idiot is. It's an art to be an idealist, boy, don't knock it."

"How do you feel about the surveys, Hugh?"

"Best salary I ever had," Hugh said.

"That's all?"

"That's something when you're forty-seven years old, that's a lot. I spent ten years dissecting frogs for college girls, and after that Mr. Wilson is a joy to behold."

"Do you think he's really dedicated?"

"In his way," Hugh said. "He's dedicated to Ira Wilson. Senator McCarthy flew high on Communist witch hunts, Wilson intends to fly high on female hormones. He's got a good thing and he won't let go."

"But what good are the surveys? Do we really do any good?"

"It's easier reading than Chaucer. It's sex, boy, pure and simple. Women lay in bed wondering how other women are doing it and we're there to tell them."

"What do you think Wilson really thinks about sex?" David asked.

"You ain't the only one wondering that," Hugh said with a chuckle.

"What?"

"That girl there, the one in the black dress. She's been standing there for a half hour letting him get a good look. The others come and go, but she just sticks there. Jesus, what a pair on her! She's giving him the full treatment, like dangling a fly near a trout."

"She's a beautiful girl," David said.

"Yep, and hot as a cracker. I spent ten years in the area of that kind of thermal radiation, and I'd know that look anywhere. Methinks Dr. Wilson might just become one of his own statistics before we leave this happy town."

David laughed. "You know, Hugh," he said, "you've always amazed me with your outlook on things. Nothing seems to bother you. Life seems to fit you and you wear it like an old shoe."

"I have my bad moments," Hugh said, "but mostly you're right. I believe in a lot of things, but mostly I believe in my own insignificance. Because of its relative size and density the human being displaces a certain amount of the earth's atmosphere for a certain amount of time. During this short duration of vegetation it busies itself with the creation of superfluous bric-a-brac like building bridges and the like and feeling superior to other forms of life. I find it impossible to take anything that simple too seriously. I'm here, I live, I busy myself, that's all."

"Do you believe in God?"

"In my own ridiculous way."

"How come you never married?"

"I did when I was much younger. It was disaster. The moment I turned away from the altar I felt mummified. Six months later I arose from the tomb."

"Were you ever in love?"

"Once, when I was teaching, but she was …" Hugh paused and stared. "Well, I'll be damned," he said, "that's her."

"Who?" David followed the line of Hugh's stare, saw an attractive auburn-haired woman in a white dress.

"The one I was in love with," Hugh said. "Well, I'll be go to hell, imagine that." His face broke into a broad grin. "I never thought that *I'd* be one of the statistics." He jammed his pipe into his pocket. "Keep the home fires burning, old pal," he said, winking. He started off through the crowd, leaving David to stare after him in astonishment.

Sylvia Thompson was aware that a good percentage of the husbands in the room had difficulty keeping their eyes off of her. A number of them had given up trying and were just staring. It amused her, but did not interest her.

The black cocktail dress she wore was designed specifically on the premise—If ya got 'em, show 'em. The skirt billowed over a series of crinoline petticoats, but the bodice was skin tight and constructed to push the breasts up. The square neck was cut back on the sides to exhibit as much of the breasts as the law allowed. On Sylvia's extraordinary development the effect was startling.

She had positioned herself on the fringe of people paying homage to Ira Wilson. She made certain that he saw her. Her occasional glances in his direction told her that he had gotten the message, but he was bridling against the obvious. This served to support her earlier theory about him, and she enjoyed the thought.

For a moment Wilson was standing alone, so she moved in. She stood before him and said, "We haven't met, Dr. Wilson, my name is Sylvia Thompson."

Wilson reddened slightly and kept his eyes up with effort. "My pleasure," he said.

"We never had an expert on sex with us before," she said, "even though most of the men here might disagree." When Wilson smiled, but did not answer, she said, "Do you practice what you preach, Doctor?"

"I'm not a preacher, Mrs. Thompson."

"Miss," Sylvia said.

"Sorry," Wilson said.

"So am I," Sylvia said. "Are you married, Doctor?"

"No, I'm not."

"Well, how fortunate," Sylvia said.

A new group of worshippers moved in around Sylvia. She smiled. "I hope to see you again, Doctor," she said.

Wilson smiled nervously and nodded. Sylvia backed out of the group and moved away. So far, so good. He's scared to death of me, but the fact that he had to keep his hands behind his back means something. She felt smugly sure of herself. It was a new experience for her, having a man within a mile who wasn't ready to leap. She went towards the TV room to have her drink replenished.

Elizabeth Pennington stood alone. Brad had been taken in tow by George Bedlow, an account exec for a rival agency, and he was in the kitchen. She noticed the man coming towards her. He was a stranger, and since she knew the complete roster of the Village Association, he must be one of Dr. Wilson's associates. He certainly looked the part with the gray hair and the tweed suit that could stand a pressing. But there was something familiar about him and it was obvious that he was making a direct line towards her and he had a broad smile on his face.

"Elizabeth!" he said when he was close enough. The voice was deep and warm and her puzzlement turned to surprise. Her mouth opened and she caught her breath.

"Hugh," Elizabeth said in a whisper.

"What a wonderful surprise," he said. "Eighteen years."

"I'm stunned," Elizabeth said. "I don't know quite what to say."

"I was right," Hugh said. "Remember the time I said that you were a pretty girl, but you'd grow into a beautiful woman? Well, by God, you've gone and done it."

"Oh, Hugh," Elizabeth said, "This is so wonderful. Are you with Dr. Wilson?"

"Yes, indeed. When you left school to get married I just gave up."

"That's not true."

"Almost. Except that I took ten years to get up enough nerve to leave."

"You haven't changed a bit," Elizabeth said.

"I have retained my wit," Hugh said, "but everything else is changed. The hair is gray and my daily diet has changed from red meat to pills and vitamins, blood builders, gas relievers, lining soothers and tranquilizers. In short, young lady, I have become an old man."

"You were an old man then."

"Thank you."

Elizabeth laughed. "I mean, really, you were all of twenty-nine, a man of the World."

"Twenty-nine. My God, was I ever only twenty-nine?"

"How about me? I was eighteen."

"You make me sound like an aging lecher."

Elizabeth laughed again. "Oh, Hugh, there has never been anyone else since who could make me laugh the way you used to. I mean happy laugh, good-feeling laugh."

"Or cry?"

Elizabeth sobered and her expression was wistful. "I did cry, didn't I? No, I never cried like that again, either. I've cried because I was hurt or unhappy, and then I've felt foolish about it. It was different, somehow."

"The sweet sadness," Hugh said. "To cry for something that should be, but isn't or can't be, is like pleading. It has a deeper meaning than the crying of self-pity. It has a place, and it merely soothes instead of making you feel ridiculous."

"The sweet sadness," Elizabeth repeated. "I like that, Hugh, because that's the way it was. It was just saying goodbye to something that had been very beautiful."

"I've never forgotten it," Hugh said.

They were jostled in the press of the crowd and Hugh spilled his drink. "Damn," he muttered.

"Let's get out of here," Elizabeth said. "There's breathing room down by the pool and I want to hear everything about you."

They angled towards the door, finally made it to the patio, then walked slowly across the close-cropped lawn towards the pool.

Sam Masserly did not like parties, nor could he see how they could have any bearing on his job. It was Cora's idea that participation in community social life was an absolute necessity for a college instructor. Bucks County parties were the easiest for Sam because he did not have to participate beyond having his body in attendance and a glass in his hand. But this particular party held a strangeness for him.

On one side of the room Cora was in animated conversation with Farley Dunham, the writer. On the other side of the room, sitting on a sofa and talking with a young French artist named Emile, was Beverly. It was the first time Sam had seen them at the same time.

Beverly, Sam imagined, must be getting the better conversation. He glanced at Cora, noticed that she was doing more listening then talking. That figured. Despite his own inclinations towards writing, Sam disliked writers. Farley Dunham was tall and thin and he slouched. His hair was short-cropped and a heavy, untrimmed mustache covered the upper lip under the thin, long nose. Dunham, Sam knew, affected a rough, ungrammatical speech that went with the biography notes on his books. He talked about his railroad days, his construction days, the period of finding himself, and he was an incredible bore. Beverly, on the other hand, was laughing and sharing the conversation about—well, whatever it is that French artists talk about.

The comparison between the two women was interesting. There was Cora, a complete phoney, a shrewish bitch, talking with that paperbacked creep just because he was supposed to be successful. And there was Beverly, being herself, her wonderful, sincere, beautiful self.

Sam felt that he was looking into a shop window. There was his wife, who was not going to be his wife for damned long, and there was the girl he wanted. He wondered how he would tell this to Cora. He had thought about it the night before as they sat in the living room. He had even put down his book and was about to speak, but when he looked up at her, he couldn't say it. It had occurred to him that she would merely laugh at him and refuse to get a divorce. What would he do if she refused? He had been doing what Cora said for so long that he wasn't certain how to go about defying her. So he had picked up his book and resumed reading. When he was with Beverly it seemed too simple. He was quite brave about it then, felt like a man. In Cora's presence it was a different matter, and he hated to admit to himself that he was actually afraid of her.

I'll work it out, he said to himself, it will take a bit of time, but I'll work it out.

Claire Roberts was afraid. She stood listening to Morley Callahan extoll the artistic merits of his latest industrial film, but her eyes were on her husband.

Mike had intercepted Sylvia Thompson as she crossed the room and he was staring with unabashed interest at the brazen female's decolleté. There was certainly nothing subtle about Mike. From the variety of facial expressions, Claire could pretty much figure out what he was saying. But the proposition received a disinterested reception and whatever it was that Sylvia had said, it wasn't flattering. When the girl moved off, Mike was left with a deep scowl marring his face.

Claire hoped that it hadn't been some insult regarding Mike's physical prowess. Like most men who are narcissistic about their bodies, Mike was secretly afraid of impotence. To them brute strength is maleness. It would never occur to Mike that a woman might respond physically to tenderness. He was never interested in mating with a woman. His pleasure was to have her ecstatic because of his stimulation. Mike was surly and difficult if anything seemed to threaten this male worship, and a remark from a woman to suggest that she might not be eager to submit to him would make him morose.

And now Mike was staring across the room at Beverly, and the look on his face made Claire afraid.

When Hugh Bascomb walked away, David was left alone. He went to the bar for a drink, then walked out to the patio and stood for a few moments listening to the Dixieland. He decided that the musicians would be better off playing fox-trots. Their interpretation of Dixie was too polite, and he liked more "gut-bucket" on the slide trombone.

He went back inside and watched the guests with a sense of detachment. Since Agatha Kelsey had been the main recruiter for the interviews, David felt that he could safely predict that most of the women in the room would record their sex histories in the next week. Here in public, in the safe area of the crowd, the drink, the platitude, there was no indication of the private hells they dwelled in. The cocktail dresses were brave armor. How many of them faced the nakedness of the marriage bed with the trembling horror of the victim being led to the guillotine? Which divorcee, now laughing, cried herself to sleep? Which one was the frigid wife who would stammer through the story of the uncle who crawled into her bed? Which one was the perfect wife and mother who dreamed of an affair with a truck driver?

By the end of the week it would all be recorded, and David would once again leave a town wondering how in hell's name so many people could make such an ungodly mess of their lives through the simple device of choosing a mate. If only a man and woman would mate for the simple reasons of desire and love it might be different, but there were so many other factors involved.

A woman might feel she was in love with a man, but it was impossible to see the man through the forest of social adornments. A woman married a social position, a career, security, a salary, many things, but seldom a man. These were the accouterments of the "good" marriage, but even on bedsheets of finest damask linen the sweating gyrations of procreation boiled down to basics of naked man and naked woman, and without the sanctity of pure love it is animal rutting.

Against this background of social marriage, a girl like Athena Wells was a paragon of virtue. She would be ostracized by polite society, but only because she threatened the structure of anti-love with her honest acceptance of love. She had knowingly taken the seed of love into her womb and nurtured it there, walked heavy-bellied through the love-hostile town safe in her world-woman knowledge of love, suffering gratefully the body-wracking pains of birth necessary to bring the screaming reality of love fulfilled from her loins. The frustrated whore-wives would hate her when they should envy her and emulate her. She was woman, the symbol, as natural as the earth is the mother birthing the Oak.

The jabbering, gesticulating scene in the room before him took on the appearance of mummery and David saw everyone wearing a mask, talking to suppress their real anxieties, hopeful that the masks would contain the real selves beneath. He felt closed-in and nervous, and he had to get away.

Putting his glass down on a table, David left the house. He had come with Hugh, but he assumed that his friend would have little trouble getting a ride back to the Inn, and he did not want to bother trying to find him. He crossed the patio, went up the flagstone walk to the swooping driveway. Cars lined the driveway on both sides. He walked along in the darkness, feeling a sense of relief.

He had difficulty getting his car out of the parking place, and when he had it on the drive, decided to back out to the road rather than chance a jam of cars at the circle near the house. It was a hundred yards to the road, but the moon was up and he maneuvered without difficulty.

When the car was heading away from the party he felt a sense of purpose and urgency, almost akin to escape, and he had to chide himself to keep the speed down.

Entering the town limits of Walkers Ferry, he cut off the highway and swooped down the narrow channel of Ferry Street. He braked hard and turned into the parking lot at the Ferry Inn.

There were two tables of late diners in the garden and Athena stood on the fringe of the dining area. David went to her, walked into her smile.

"When do you finish?" he asked.

"They're the last two tables," she said. "A half hour, I guess."

"May I wait for you?"

"I'd be disappointed if you didn't," she said. "How was your party?"

"Grim," David said, "absolutely grim. I missed you every minute."

"Hmmm, pretty words. You probably couldn't take your eyes off Sylvia Thompson."

"Who?"

Athena laughed lightly. "I forget that you're new around here," she said. "Sylvia has the record bust in Walkers Ferry."

"I saw her," David said.

"You can't miss her."

"Do I hear a purr?" David asked.

"You do indeed. A purr of envy. Pardon me." She left his side and walked to one of the tables where a stout man was signalling for his check.

David turned and opened the door behind him. He entered the barroom and went to the bar, taking a stool near the end. He ordered Irish Whisky on the rocks.

The tables in the garden emptied on his second drink and he saw Athena clearing away the dishes. He glanced at the clock, toyed with his drink, lit a cigarette, killed time.

Athena came into the bar. She wore a full cotton print skirt that lashed about her legs as she walked, a simple short-sleeved blouse and leather thong sandals. Her thick coil of honey-blonde hair was doubled and fixed atop her head. She wore no lipstick and her eyes were ringed with a thin line of black, making them stand out startlingly blue against the cream texture of her skin. David slid off the stool, nodded to the bartender, and took her arm. They smiled together without speaking, went to the door and out into the night.

"Do we walk tonight?" David asked.

"Not tonight. Let's just go to my place and we'll listen to music."

"We drive?"

"It's only a block," Athena said.

They walked up Ferry street, crossed the canal bridge. They passed the office of the Justice of Peace, a bookstore named "Lefty's", a Tea House that catered to the girdled gluttons who came in bus groups to browse through the town like locusts, two shops operated by respectable homosexuals, a barber shop for French poodles.

As they walked David suddenly realized that Gwen had completely left his mind. It was less than a week since he had seen her, had seriously wondered if he was in love with her, and already she was out of his life completely. Well, not completely, he reasoned. It is impossible to touch upon someone without taking something of them to heart. Even the casual acquaintance has an influence on your life, but for the future, there was no Gwen, and it seemed that he had been some other person, some stranger whom he had known.

He glanced at Athena, was taken as usual by the elfin beauty of her, but seeing her as a woman was even more exciting to him.

Just the thought that he loved her filled him with a feeling of delight. It was a wondrous warm sensation that made him glad, made him want to shout. It was like finding a treasure, like suddenly deciphering a map that he had pondered over for years. Love was like a riddle. It is baffling until you find the key, then it is astoundingly simple. Love was simply a case of finding the girl capable of receiving it.

They turned into a short side street and at the end was the small house where Athena lived with her child. Athena rang the bell and the baby-sitter came to the door.

"Hello, Martha," Athena said as they entered, "you remember Mr. Belson."

A few words about the behavior of the child and Martha gathered up her school books and left. Athena was in the kitchen making coffee, and David kneeled on the floor by the record player, shuffling through the records.

"Feel like some Bartok?" David asked.

"Not tonight," Athena said. "There's a record there of Debussy. Some of his lesser known things. Play that. It was given to me by a wonderful guy named Ed Staley who knows every note Debussy ever wrote. Come to think of it, you'll have to meet Ed. He's a rare and wonderful person."

"You're kind of rare and wonderful yourself," David said.

"Thank you, Sir."

David found the record and put it on the turntable. He listened a moment, enjoying the lyricism, then he stood up and prowled the room. It was a small house. The living room, a small kitchen, two bedrooms on either side of a narrow hall. The living room contained a modern sofa, two sling chairs, a long coffee table and a number of cushions for sitting on the floor. David sat on the sofa, tapped a cigarette from the pack, lit it.

"I like your house," David said.

"You said that the other night."

"And you said it was too small."

"Yes," Athena said, coming in from the kitchen, "and it is. One small boy can make it very small in about five minutes."

"When am I going to see that boy?"

"One day, maybe."

"Maybe? Don't you want me to see him?"

"I'm not sure," Athena said. "Little boys are impressionable, David. I don't want Dougie to have a series of 'Uncles'. If I date someone, that's one thing. I know that one day whoever he is won't be coming back, and that's all right. It might not be so easy for Doug."

She was sitting on a cushion in front of him, her legs curled back, the skirt spread around her. He leaned towards her. "I love you, Athena," he said.

She returned his steady gaze. "Don't joke, David, that's not something I take lightly."

"I'm not joking, Athena, I love you." There was gravity in his voice and he did not take his eyes from hers. She looked at him for what seemed like an interminably long time.

"I think I love you, too, David," she said. "I'm not sure, but I think I do." She got to her feet and went to the kitchen. In a moment, she came back. "The coffee can keep," she said.

Pushing a cushion around, she dropped on her knees before him. "Have you ever had the responsibility of having someone deeply in love with you?"

"I make—"

"I'm not talking about money, David. There's a much more difficult responsibility. You're a good person, I know that. There is an emotional responsibility you accept when you accept love. It hangs in a delicate balance, but it can become awfully heavy. When I love, I love for keeps."

"I love you," David said, "I want to marry you."

Athena looked up at him with questioning intensity. "I don't know, David," she said. "I think that you know that you want to marry, but I'm not certain that you want to marriage.

The distance between marrying and marriaging is wide. One is the impulse of the moment. It is simple. The other is two people being so close that they lose their indentities as individuals and exist as one mind in two bodies."

"Are you certain that's the way it should be?" David asked.

"It has to be," she said.

"I'm not sure. I like to think of marriage as two ships traveling separately to the same destination. If the ships were lashed together a rough sea would destroy them."

Athena mulled his words in silence. She glanced down at her hands. "I don't know, David. Putting this into words gets it all confused."

"I love you, Athena. You can't be confused about that."

She looked up. "I asked you once if you had ever been in love," she said.

"I can't answer that," he said. "At the time I thought that I was. It was never like this, but maybe it is a matter of degree. I could have been in love, but not deeply enough."

"Do you know what the feeling is?"

"Yes. You feel it in the heart."

"But the heart is just an organ, a part of the body for pumping the blood through the body."

"That's true, but there's something else. It defies science to explain it, but it exists. Athena, let me try to explain this with an example. I have this friend, a good, close friend. He's an intellectual, somewhat of a cynic. But not too long ago his wife died suddenly. I was with him when it happened and afterwards we were driving away from the hospital and he was talking. One thing he said really hit me. It was about the heart being just another organ of the body, but he also said that the pain hit him squarely in the heart, a heavy ache that made him grimace. Why the heart? Why not the liver or the kidney? I know that psychologists scoff at the existence of such a thing as the soul, but there must be something to the poetic premise that love exists in the heart, just as there must be a soul in the human body that is divorced from the mind. I love you, Athena, and at this moment it is as if a wire noose is being pulled tight around my heart. That's all I can say. I love you."

Athena swallowed and her eyes misted. "David," she said, "I'm going to stand up. I don't want you to kiss me. I want you to lift me and carry me into the bedroom. I don't want to walk there as though this were a prearranged assignation, I want you to take me there, to carry me. I want to lie next to you in the dark with nothing between us. I want to hold you, listen to your heart beat. I want you to make love to me, make love *with* me, and then we'll know." She got to her feet.

David was trembling as he stood and lifted her into his arms.

CHAPTER ELEVEN

Cora Masserly parked her car on South Main Street and walked to the Town Hall. She checked her watch and noted that she was on time for the appointment.

Cora stepped into the musty hallway where a desk had been placed and where a tidy, officious woman now sat. "I'm Cora Masserly," she said, approaching the desk.

"You're here for the interview," Rita Talbot said, glancing along her list of names.

"Yes."

"Hmmmm. Here you are." Rita made a check after the name on the list, then got to her feet. "Come with me, please."

The hallway was uncarpeted and their heels clacked on the hard wood. There were two closed doors on either side of the hallway. Rita went to the last door on the right, opened it, and stood aside for Cora to enter.

The room was square and small. Just beyond the door was a small table holding a pad and pencil and an ashtray. A wooden chair with curving arms faced the table. On the ceiling of the room hung a portable light fixture which contained four bright spotlights. The lights shone on the young man who was seated behind a table on which were a pile of forms and a number of pencils stuffed into a jar.

"You will sit right here, Mrs. Masserly," Rita said, indicating the empty chair. "This is Mr. Belson who will interview you."

"How do you do?" Cora said.

"How do you do," David said.

Rita held the chair until Cora sat, then she turned and left the room, closing the door behind her. There was a moment of tense silence, a shuffling of the chair while Cora got comfortable.

"Your name, please."

"Cora Masserly."

"Age."

"Twenty-nine."

"Married?"

"Yes."

"Children?"

"No," Cora answered.

David nodded, then took a deep breath. "You may wonder about the spotlights, Mrs. Masserly," David said. "They are a special innovation of Dr. Wilson's. While you can see me plainly because of the intense glare, you are sitting in darkness. This gives you perfect anonymity while at the same time you will not experience the terror that generally comes with talking to a screen or a microphone. I would like to say that the questions I ask are of no interest to me personally, they are just part of the questionaire I have here in front of me. I will try to help you with any answers you find difficult. Are you ready?"

"Yes."

"Fine. Now, we'll begin with the series of questions on pre-adolescent heterosexual sex play. When did you have your first experiment with masturbation?"

Cora gasped and her eyes widened. "Are you serious?"

"Most children masturbate, Mrs. Masserly."

"Well, I certainly never did!"

David marked the answer on the form. "Did you engage in sex play with other children?"

"Never!"

David glanced up and Cora had the feeling that he could see her. This whole thing is thoroughly disgusting, she thought.

"When was the first time that you were aware of the sex act? What age?"

"What age?"

"Yes, how old were you?"

"I'm not sure." Cora scowled, and the memory came back to make her shudder. She had been spending the week at Uncle George's farm and there was that beautiful sorrel mare and then that day that she had stood by the fence and had seen the stallion chase the mare and the way the mare screamed and kicked, but the stallion stayed there, and she had run back to the barn to tell Uncle George that the stallion was stuck to the mare and he had laughed.

Her face reddened and she felt the same disgust as before. "I ... I'm not sure," Cora said. "I suppose it was when I was ten."

"What were the circumstances?"

Cora's hand trembled. She had inched the chair forward unconsciously and her breasts touched the edge of the table. "A girl in school told me," she said. That was Gladys. What was her last name?

"In what way were you told?"

"In what way?"

"Yes, how did this girl explain it?"

Cora swallowed hard. What could this have to do with her sex life? "She ... she said that she knew where babies came from," Cora said. "She said that boys urinated on girls and this made babies." And that same week Cora had gone with Gladys to the old Canby house and Jerry Graham was waiting and they had crawled under the house and she watched Jerry do it to Gladys and then they said that they would tell her Mother unless she let Jerry do it to her and she was so frightened that she let him and she didn't feel anything even though Gladys said it was fun and then she thought sure that she would have a baby and she cried in bed that night because she didn't want a baby and she told her

Mother and she was beaten with a strap and told that she was filthy.

"Did you experiment with any boys at this time?" David asked.

"Really!" Cora said in a shocked voice. "What a thing to ask. Why that's a positively filthy thought!"

"I'm sorry," David said. He made notations on the form, wondering what made this woman frigid, feeling a bit sorry for her husband, but also feeling sorry for her. "We'll go on now to premarital sex," he said.

While Hugh Bascomb could not see the woman, he remembered her from the party when Elizabeth had pointed her out, and he also remembered seeing her in a number of movies. He looked at the form, surprised that she was forty-six because she had looked much younger, still beautiful, but in a more sedate way. He had been through a number of questions. Claire Roberts had been an early experimenter in the rites of sexual pleasure.

"Did you have sexual relations with the opposite sex prior to marriage?"

"Yes," Claire said, twisting her handkerchief. Damn, she thought, why am I nervous?

"At what age?"

"I was ..." She thought a moment. "I believe I was thirteen." My God, she thought, I was just a baby! Beverly is twenty and I think she's still a virgin.

"Did you experience pleasure at that time?"

"Yes." Did I? God, it was wonderful. I thought I was going to go crazy. It was that big guy who worked on the same drilling gang as Dad. I was scared to death at first, because he was so big and all, but after that first terrible hurt, it was wonderful. That was the end of playing with dolls for me!

"Have you always received satisfaction in the sexual act?"

"Yes." Well, not always. There was that time with old man Ruebens when I was fourteen and had to have that party dress in his window. But, of course, that was a different kind of satisfaction when I realized I could have anything I wanted if I was smart about it.

"Between the first time and your marriage, how many partners did you have?"

Claire took a deep breath. "I'm not certain," she said.

"Take your time," Hugh said, "try to recall."

Claire picked up the pencil on the table before her and made scratches on the pad. About a dozen before she entered that first beauty contest. There had been four judges and she had to take on three of them. And then there had been other beauty contests and agents for modeling jobs and photographers who would make up your portfolio without charge if you were friendly. What could this man know about being hungry and poor and wanting to be somebody important? What else do you do when you're a girl and all you've got to get ahead on is the fact that you're a girl and beautiful and men want you? Dammit, what else do you do? You flop on your back and spread your legs, that's what! She had to suppress a giggle when she remembered the famous actress who once said to her, 'I'm just damn glad we're not like those old time western gun fighters. If I had a notch on my ass for every man I had to knock off to get where I am, they'd call me the Corduroy Kid.' There must have been more than a hundred men, she thought. It never occured to me to count them before. It's almost sickening when you think of them in numbers like that. I never thought of myself as being immoral. I had to do it, that's all. I had to do it, just like Beverly will never have to do!

"I'm not sure," she said in answer to the question. "I'd guess about twenty-five." Then she felt that she could explain. "I wanted to be an actress," she said.

Claire twisted the pencil in her hands. He must think I'm an awful slut, she thought. Well, let him. I had to do what I had to do. I got where I wanted to go. I did it for my baby, and she'll never have to do it for anybody except for love.

The interviews broke off for lunch, and David walked down Main Street with Hugh Bascomb.

"How was your morning?" David asked.

"Just dandy. I'm now qualified to write the Girl's Guide on How To Be An Actress."

"Maybe you should open a school."

"I'm afraid I wouldn't have the strength. Those schools must use the couch more than a psychiatrist. How did you do?"

"Two happy, bovine housewives and one mixed up enough to make your blood run cold."

They laughed together, and when they reached the Ferry Inn, David said, "I won't be lunching with you, Hugh, I have to see someone down the street."

"That cute little blonde?"

"No, but a friend of hers."

"Well, good luck, Don Juan." Hugh turned up towards the entrance to the Inn, and David continued along Main Street.

When he reached the office of the *Register,* David went up the steps and through the door. There was no one in the office, but he heard a chair scrape behind the screen at the far end of the room. "Knox?" he said.

"Yes." Knox came from behind the screen. "Ah, David," he said, "good to see you."

"I thought we might have lunch together."

"Wonderful. I was just going to lock up and eat. I live upstairs and cook for myself. Come on, we'll open a can of soup."

They left the office, went to the side of the building and up the steep flight of stairs to the tidy three-room apartment.

"Make yourself at home," Knox said. "I'll do the kitchen chores."

David dropped into the depths of a large leather chair. He settled back and tapped a cigarette from his pack, lighting it and inhaling deeply.

Knox came from the kitchen and dropped silverware and napkins on the table. "Is this strictly a social call, or do you have something else on your mind?"

"I've decided to leave Dr. Wilson," David said.

Knox nodded his head thoughtfully. "I have anything to do with this decision?" he asked.

"A little," David said. "Mostly you've just been the catalyst to set a lot of thoughts into motion."

"You thinking of staying here?"

"I've thought of it. I want to marry Athena."

Knox raised his eyebrows, then he smiled and chuckled. "Well," he said, "this has been a week of decisions for you."

"I'm in love with her," David said.

"I would assume you'd have to be in love to marry anyone," Knox said. "Does she know this?"

"Yes."

"Have you met her child?"

"Yes."

"Then she must believe that you want to marry her," Knox said. "And you know about her past."

"She told me."

"She would. She's quite a girl."

"There's one thing I don't understand," David said. "She never says anything about this other man, but she still seems to be in love with him in some way."

"Only because he was a good man," Knox said.

"A good man? My God, Knox, he got her pregnant and didn't do anything about it! You call that a good man?"

"He didn't deny her, David. He didn't marry her, because he didn't want to marry her. He was honest with her. Marriage isn't everything. You should know that better than anyone, you who must have recorded the hundreds of lives made miserable by the simple institution of two strangers sharing bed and board when they should have had their little tumble in the hay and gone their happy ways." Knox went back to the kitchen to tend his soup, but he raised his voice to be heard. "His name was Frank and he had a business here in town. He also had a wife who hated the way a jealous woman can, and she refused to give him a divorce. But that is beside the point. He wouldn't have married Athena anyway, because they weren't suited to live together. Anyway, when Athena was pregnant with his child he recognized the fact. Most men would want to hide her or deliver her to some dirty backroom to be aborted by a rusty spoon. Frank stood by her while she had the child, and he made her walk open in the street and keep her head up. He lost his business over it." Knox came back into the room and put two bowls on the table. "What would you have done in his place, David?"

"Something stupid, I suppose. Maybe something cowardly. I don't know."

"It's hard to know," Knox said. "But he did what any man would like to think he would have the courage to do. He kept that girl's love clean. That would mean a lot to a woman, and Athena is a woman." Knox waved at the table. "Come eat."

David went to the table and they ate in silence. When Knox was finished, he asked, "Have you told Wilson?"

"I'm going to do it this evening."

"Have you given our local college some thought?"

"I drove out to see it," David said. "It's very nice. I didn't make any inquiries, though."

"If you're interested, I'll have you meet the President. He's a bit stuffy, but a nice enough person."

"I'm interested."

"The pay won't be great."

"There are other things," David said. "And now I have to get back."

"No coffee?"

"No thanks, I need steady nerves."

Sylvia Thompson smiled with pleasure when she saw that Dr. Wilson was handling her interview. She allowed Rita Talbot to seat her, then toyed with the pencil and pad and examined the man while he made his usual preamble about the lights and secrecy and his own clinical disinterest.

"May I smoke, Doctor," she asked.

"Of course, Mrs. Thompson."

"Miss," Sylvia said. "Remember, I said the same thing at the party."

Wilson coughed and made no answer, but Sylvia could see that he was remembering, not what she had said, but what she had looked like.

Wilson recorded the facts of age, marital status, education.

"Would you like my measurements, Doctor?"

"That won't be necessary," Wilson said, a look of cold disdain on his face.

Sylvia had looked Wilson up in *Who's Who* and knew his age to be 48. She liked his long hands, his wiry, sturdy build. The leaner the horse, the longer the race, she said to herself, smiling.

Wilson was asking his questions pertaining to preadolescent sex and Sylvia was answering with relish.

"The first orgasm was self-induced at the age of eight," she said. "I used my father's best meerchaum pipe. I hated the sonofabitch and it made me laugh every time I saw him smoke it after that."

Wilson scowled and his fingers whitened on the pencil, but he kept his voice steady and asked, "How would you define foreplay?"

"Does that mean having someone finger you?"

"Is that what it means to you?"

"I guess it means all the stuff a man will do to get you hot. Frankly, Doctor, I've never needed any. When I'm ready to go, I go."

"Have you ever achieved satisfaction through petting?"

"Not me," she said. "I always had to have the real thing. I guess you might say I was precocious."

When Wilson reached the section dealing with premarital intimacies, Sylvia leaned back in the chair and lit another cigarette.

"Look at it this way, Doctor," she said. "I got bounced the first time when I was fifteen and I had to use will power to wait until then. I always needed it. I was a healthy young girl. I never thought it was bad and I still don't. It's a function like anything else. I have no idea how many men I've tumbled. I took them whenever I could get them."

"Were any of these affairs of a sustaining nature?"

"No. After a bout with me they were usually scared to death."

"What was your relationship with your father?"

"I couldn't stand the righteous bastard." Now there is an understatement, Sylvia thought. But how could you really explain that much hatred? Her father was more than stern, he acted as though the devil walked the halls of his house. Sylvia remembered the night that her mother had been thrown out of the house. She had heard angry voices from her bed, had gotten up and rushed to the hallway. At the bottom of the staircase her father stood over her mother, who was sprawled on the carpet. He was calling her foul names, then he kicked her and she screamed. That was the last time Sylvia had seen her mother, and later she learned that her father had found his wife with another man. She had been lectured and lectured on sin, but it only served to make her hate the man more. I paid him back, Sylvia thought, I paid that bastard back in spades. I became the worst slut in that damn town. And every boy and man she knew was the image of the father, and she relished the hold she had over them in their lust.

"Have you been married?" Wilson asked.

"Three times." And everyone of them was as righteous as that bastard.

"How often did you have intimate relations with your husbands?"

"Every night at first. Sometimes in the mornings. But they generally begged off after awhile." God, the way she used to taunt them—anything to make them realize that they weren't men. The worst part was when it was over and she couldn't stand to have them near her, and she didn't make any bones about telling them. How she avenged her mother! How she hated them, how she hated them all!

Elizabeth Pennington was startled when she entered the room and saw Hugh Bascomb sitting behind the table under the bright lights. She took her chair and saw Hugh stiffen when Rita Talbot announced her name.

When Rita left the room, Hugh said, "You don't have to go through with this, Liz. I'll have one of the others interview you."

"No," Elizabeth said, "I have nothing to hide." She added to herself, not from you, anyway.

Hugh went through the questions about preadolescent sex, recorded a natural sexual interest. He had to chuckle over the incident in the football stadium.

"It wasn't funny at the time," Elizabeth said.

"I'm sorry," Hugh said.

"I hated sex until I met you."

"Hmmmm, yes, well." He cleared his throat. "Am I next?"

"Yes."

He smiled. "This is a bit irregular," he said.

"Well," Elizabeth said with an edge of irritation, "I don't do this every day myself."

Hugh sobered. "I think I'll just skip on to your marriage. But I do want to say, off the record, that I made love to you with love.

There hasn't been any love since." He coughed. "Okay, on to marriage. What is the frequency of love-making in your marriage at present?"

Elizabeth bit her lip. She hadn't thought about it so coldly. Putting love into figures made it distasteful. When was the last time with Brad? Three weeks. And before that? "It's … its about once a month. I mean, it's because Brad is away most of the time."

"He's home on week-ends?"

Elizabeth realized that this was not one of the printed questions, but she felt compelled to answer, to make some rational excuse for her marriage. "He's very tired most of the time." It was a lame excuse. Hugh had met Brad at the party and he was certainly lively enough, and Hugh had been to the house for Sunday dinner and Brad had spent the afternoon playing tennis with Debbie. But later, in bed, he had again begged off on the excuse that he was tired.

"Do you reach a climax in your love-making?"

"Yes … usually … I mean, well, sometimes I don't."

"Do you know why you don't?"

"I don't know … I mean … that's a difficult question. How should I … well, yes, I know. Dammit, it's because I know he's not interested. That he's just doing it to keep me quiet!"

Hugh looked hard at her, then he bent back to the questionaire and tried to keep his approach more clinical.

"Since you have been married, have you engaged in any extramarital relationship?"

"Once." Elizabeth bit her lip because she saw the surprise register on his face.

"When was that?"

"Last week."

"Last week?"

Elizabeth swallowed hard and clenched her fists. She had no idea that this was going to be so difficult. "Oh, Hugh," she said, "it was horrible." The tears spilled from her eyes, running the mascara down her cheeks. In jerky sentences she related the incident with Chet Parker. Before she could finish Hugh was at her side, holding her arms. She rose from the chair and leaned against him. "Oh, Hugh," she cried, "what am I going to do? I'm so miserable!"

CHAPTER TWELVE

David stood in front of the closed door. His tongue flicked over his lips and he squared his shoulders. He lifted his fist and knocked.

"Come in."

Opening the door, David stepped into the room. Dr. Wilson was standing at the table which had been put into the room, and Rita Talbot was shuffling questionnaires into an orderly pile.

"Hello, David," Wilson said. "That will be all, Rita."

"Yes, Sir," Rita Talbot said. She nodded at David as she left the room, closing the door after her.

"Well, David," Wilson said, rubbing his hands together, "It's been a productive day. I always feel good at the end of the day, as though another brick has been cemented into an important monument."

"There's something I wanted to speak to you about, Sir," David said.

Wilson's expression changed, as though he was suddenly thrown on the defensive, and his eyes were wary. "What is it?"

"I want to submit my resignation," David said.

Wilson pursed his lips. One hand came up and rubbed the side of his face. "I see," he said. "You have the offer of a better position?"

"No, Sir, it's nothing like that. It's just that ... well, Sir, I just don't believe in the work any longer."

Wilson looked as though he had been struck in the face. "I don't understand," he said with effort.

"Well," David said, "when I first began this work I felt that we were doing something important, something good. Now I don't believe that."

"What *do* you believe, David?"

"I believe that what we're doing is destructive. I think we're little better than peeping toms. Everytime I complete a questionnaire I feel as though I have just opened an ugly sore, not to cleanse the wound or heal it, but just to open it to see the color of the puss inside."

Wilson whirled abruptly and went to the window, his back to David. The muscles stood out in his neck like thin rope and his hands were clenched. "That's clear enough," he said. "I accept your resignation." His voice was cold.

"I'll complete the survey here," David said.

"I'd rather you didn't. I don't believe I could trust your work, David, after what you've said."

"I'm sorry, Sir."

"Don't be sorry for me, David, only for yourself and your obviously narrow vision." He turned and his eyes glistened. "It is our *duty* to expose the puss, as you put it! If there is evil locked in the breast of women, and we have proved that there is, then it is our duty to show it to the world!" His jaw jutted. "Goodbye, David."

David watched the man turn his arched back away, ending the interview, and for a moment he felt that he was in the presence of a madman. There was nothing more to say. It was done, over with. Turning, David went to the door and opened it. He stepped into the hallway and closed the door.

Going down the stairs, David peered into the bar. He saw Knox Martin alone at a table. He entered and went to the table.

"David," Knox said.

"Hello, Knox, may I join you?"

"Please."

David took a chair on the opposite side of the table and sat down. "I just told Wilson I was resigning."

"How did he take it?"

"Not well."

"A general hates to have his lieutenants desert him," Knox said. "He'll get over it."

"Knox," David said, "there's one curious thing. In the conversation up there just now I had the feeling that Wilson hates women. I mean really despises them."

"That's possible."

"But if he's conducting the surveys on the basis of hatred the whole program is vicious. How could he get into this line of work?"

"It compensates," Knox said. "Beethoven wrote militant music and he was a coward. Nietzsche believed in the super race and he was a physical misfit. All things are relative. The Marquis de Sade wrote that a sadist gives extreme pleasure to a masochist."

"But if that's the case then something should be done about it."

"You've done all you can," Knox said. "You got out of it."

"But—"

"David, don't fight it. Have a drink, have dinner, be glad that your ideals are intact. Evil has a way of destroying itself. There are those who believe that good always triumphs. This is never the case. Morality is steady and complacent and safe and it lasts. Evil is born in passion and it rages until it has run the gamut and is consumed in its own flames. Good has nothing to do with it."

The heavy chords of Beethoven's Fifth Symphony rumbled through the house. Hugh Bascomb seated on a divan in the living room, looked up as Elizabeth came into the room.

"I guess Debbie isn't going to get home for dinner," Elizabeth said. "We may as well eat."

Hugh gulped the last of his martini, put the glass down and got to his feet. He followed Elizabeth into the dining room where three places had been set at the long, rectangular table.

"Sit at the end, there," Elizabeth said. "I'll bring everything in."

Hugh busied himself with uncorking and pouring the wine while Elizabeth brought the several dishes to the table, then they sat facing each other. Hugh lifted his wine glass. "To old times," he said.

Elizabeth smiled. "Which is now a matter of record."

"We were going to forget all that," Hugh said.

"Yes, but I can't."

"No, I guess not. We never ever forget the things we do. They pass out of the mind for a time, but they're always there, lurking for the inopportune time to come popping up."

Elizabeth did not answer and they ate in silence for some minutes. Finally, Hugh asked, "Do you eat alone often?"

"Quite a bit, but you have to realize that Debbie is a teenager. She has friends of her own and she spends a good bit of time with them."

"Brad couldn't commute?"

"He did for awhile," she said, "but it was awfully hard on him."

"In other words, he would rather stay in New York."

"Really, Hugh, this doesn't concern you."

"Have you thought of getting a divorce?"

"No," she said abruptly.

"Why not?"

"I don't know why you ... Oh, I don't know." She put her fork down and took a gulp of the wine. "I know my marriage is a failure, but I don't want to admit failure. And I have Debbie to think about."

"She doesn't know about you and Brad?"

"She ... well, I'm not sure."

"Then she does know."

"She knows something is wrong, yes, but ... Oh, Hugh, what is the point of all this talk?"

"No point, I guess. It's just that I'd like to see the woman I've always loved in a happy situation."

Elizabeth lowered her eyes to her plate and her voice was small when she said, "Thank you, Hugh."

Hugh stared at her in silence, then he lifted his glass. "Another toast," he said. Elizabeth looked up. "To keeping my mouth shut," he said.

"I'll drink to that," Elizabeth said.

Claire Roberts was still disturbed by the morning interview, and now, at dinner, Mike was taunting her.

"How did the scientific mind react to all the shocking details?" he asked.

"I don't know what you mean," Claire said, toying with her food.

"How about positions? Did you tell them your favorite?"

"Mike, really!"

"The Roberts family at home," Beverly said. "Frank discussions at the dinner table. Do you think you might get your mind out of the gutter while we eat, Mr. Roberts?"

"The gutter?" Mike said. "I was talking about your Mother."

"You don't have to twist what I say, Big Man. I was talking about your mind."

"How come you didn't get interviewed?" Mike asked.

"Because I wasn't interested," Beverly said.

"Afraid they might find something out?"

"That's none of your damn business!"

"Please," Claire said. "Mike, talk about something else. This is really very dull."

"Sex is dull? Since when?"

"I don't mean that," Claire said. "I mean—"

"She means she'd like to eat her soup in peace," Beverly said. "It's bad enough sitting and looking at you without having to listen to your gutter tongue."

Mike dropped his fork on the plate and his eyes narrowed with anger. "You think I'm out of the gutter, huh?"

"It shows, Buster, I don't have to think," Beverly said.

"You figure you're better than me, huh?"

"That's a laugh!"

"And better than your Mother," Mike said.

"I didn't say anything about my—"

"I said it!" Mike snapped the words through his teeth. "You're a gutter kid, and don't you forget it! If I walked in the gutter, your Mother laid in it!"

"Mike!" Claire cried.

"Shut up!" He pointed his finger at Beverly. "You're the same flesh and blood as your Mother, girlie, and your Mother ain't no angel!"

Beverly leaped to her feet, the tears had started in her eyes. "I won't listen to this!"

"You don't have to because you know it's true! You wanta hear how I met your Mother? You wanta hear it?"

"I don't want to hear anything from you again!" Beverly shouted. "Your voice makes me sick! You've got a rotten mind, and I can't stand being under the same roof with you!" She turned and ran from the room.

Mike Roberts sat back. He was breathing heavily and his mouth was twisted into a snarl.

"You didn't have to say that," Claire said.

"It's the truth!" Mike snarled. "You're a tramp! I know it, just like everybody else knows it! I'm sick of that damn kid of yours treating me like dirt!"

Claire got up from her chair. "You are dirt," she said softly.

Mike spun out of his chair. A constricted cry of rage rose from his throat. He lurched forward, swinging his arm. His open palm cracked against the side of Claire's face, snapping her head back. She cried out in surprise and pain. She was knocked off balance, and Mike swept his arm around again, back-handing her across the mouth. She staggered away and fell to her knees. Mike came to her. He jerked her head up by her hair. "Don't say that to me, you two-bit whore!" He smashed his fist into her mouth and let her drop to the carpet. "That'll teach you," he growled, "and I'm gonna teach that kid, too."

Claire whimpered, but she did not move. The blood trickled from the corner of her mouth.

Sam Masserly could not get his mind on the book. The page was a blur of gray. He looked across at Cora who was knitting. How was he going to tell her? It had to come out, sooner or later. He knew that he couldn't go on meeting Beverly without the town knowing about it, and there was always some helpful soul who would be on the telephone to let poor dear Cora know about it. Beverly was right. What they felt for each other had to be exposed to the sun. But how could he tell Cora? Damn, this was a helluva lot more difficult than he had thought it would be.

The telephone rang, startling him, and he began to get up.

"I'll get it," Cora said. She put her knitting aside and went to the hallway. She felt uneasy for some reason she could not fathom, but she had decided that it was because of Sam's strangeness, and while she had sat knitting, she had been plotting some method of making him tell her what it was all about. She lifted the receiver and held it to her ear.

"Yes?" she said.

"Cora? This is Marcia."

"Oh."

"Still mad at me?"

"I hadn't thought about it," Cora said.

"I'm glad. Look, Hon, I've missed you, and I wanted to apologize for the other day. I guess it was the brandy."

"It doesn't matter," Cora said.

"Good. I knew you'd understand. Look, Cora, there's a party on tonight up on Temperance Hill."

Cora frowned. She had heard some wild stories about Temperance Hill—the name given to an area North of the town where a group of New Yorkers owned houses and did considerable drinking. She had never been on the Hill, but she knew that the houses were expensive and extremely private. "I'm sorry," she said, eager to end the conversation, "Sam and I are staying in tonight."

"Come on," Marcia said. "Don't be a sober-sides. This is strictly a hen party. You'll love it. Let Sam stay home. I'll come by and pick you up."

"No thanks," Cora said. "I really don't feel like it."

"Okay," Marcia said, "suit yourself. But I'll be here until nine. Give me a call if you change your mind."

"Goodbye," Cora said. "Thanks for calling." She cradled the phone and went back to the living room. She hadn't told the interviewer anything about Marcia. When the question had been raised she had felt a moment of panic. She didn't know why.

David turned the car off River Road and the headlights swept up the steep incline of Jericho Hill.

"It was nice of Knox to loan you his car," Athena said. She sat against the door with her body turned so that she could look at David.

"Now that I'm unemployed I don't have the use of the company car," he said. "How does it feel to be with one of the vast army of the unemployed?"

"Feels fine to me," Athena said. "How do you feel about it?"

"I feel the way a catholic must feel when he has left the confessional, lit six candles and said twenty Hail Marys. If I have sinned, and that's possible, I at least have the feeling that my sins have been neatly bundled, that as far as that set of sins is concerned, they're finished."

"That's not very scientific."

"You're right. It's a complete rationalization, but it makes me feel better, and tonight I want to feel better. Do you realize that this is our first real, official date?"

"I realize it. That's why I'm taking you to an expensive place to buy my dinner."

"And me without a job."

Athena laughed. "That's my luck. I meet a successful man, and the minute I fall in love with him he quits his job."

"Then you *are* in love with me?"

"Didn't you know?"

"Yes, I knew, but I've never heard you say it."

"Do you need reassurance?"

"Hey, now, I'm the expert at questions."

"About sex," she said. "I'm talking about love."

"You're talking about reassurance."

"I have the feeling we're not always going to agree on things," Athena said.

"We'll scandalize the neighbors with our fights," David said.

"Do I take that as a proposal?"

"You may, indeed."

"I take it and I accept. David! Watch the road!" She laughed lightly, a warm, happy laugh.

CHAPTER THIRTEEN

Sylvia Thompson made tunafish salad and ate it alone in her kitchen. She washed the meal down with brandy, left most of it on her plate and went to the living room and switched on the television, trying all the channels. It bored her and she turned the set off and went to the hi-fi set, took a handful of jazz records without looking at the titles and put them on.

Returning to the kitchen, she took the brandy bottle off the table and brought it back to the living room. She filled her glass and dropped onto the wide divan. The phonograph was turned too high, but she didn't move. The throaty baritone sax of Gerry Mulligan filled the room, seemed to make the air tremble with sensuous sound. She leaned back, closed her eyes, drank slowly.

Before the record ended she was on her feet pacing the room. God, how she hated being alone in the big house! Maybe it would be better if she sold the place and got an apartment in New York. At least she wouldn't have to be alone. The nervousness took hold of her and her skin seemed to itch with restlessness. She stopped and gulped the brandy.

She went back to the divan and dropped down. The feeling she knew so well was beginning to spread through her. She poured more brandy and gulped it. Maybe a tranquillizer would help, she thought, or a cold shower. But she knew that neither would do her any good. How long had it been since that kid cutting the grass? A week. She cupped her hands over her breasts. They felt swollen and painful.

Springing off the couch, she ran to the door and flung it open. The record continued to blare. She slammed the door after her and ran down the stone steps. Her low-slung Mercedes was in the driveway. She jerked the door open and slid under the wheel. The engine roared and the tires wailed against the macadam as she tramped the accelerator.

She kidded onto Bradley Road, shifted gears, enjoying the feeling of motion, the driving power the car gave her. She knew Wilson was staying at the Ferry Inn, and she knew that she had to have him. The righteous bastard, she'd make him crawl!

I really shouldn't drink this much, Elizabeth Pennington thought. There had been martinis and wine and now bourbon, and she was feeling the relaxed glow that always came to her with drinking.

Hugh was sitting in the easy chair adjacent to the sofa where she sat, and he was talking, but she wasn't listening to the words. She was thinking how comfortable it was to sit in a room with a man who loved you, just sit and listen to someone who was not looking at you with critical eyes. You could just relax and not give a damn about how the argument was going to start or had you said the right thing or were you really at fault or had it been a bad week at the office. And how nice that it could be Hugh. She was remembering those other years and how gentle he had been with her and how she had loved him. She recalled the ache she always felt just before she saw him, and the terrible depression she felt when he told her that he would not marry her because she was too young. And now here he was and they were in the same room and it was just like wiping out all those years between. She suddenly realized that Hugh was asking her a question.

"I didn't hear you," she said.

"I know," Hugh said. "I asked you what you were thinking."

She tilted her head and gazed at him. Yes, it was the same Hugh. "I was thinking," she said, "that if you didn't come over here and kiss me I was going to scream." Now why did I say that? she wondered.

Hugh's hands gripped the arm of the chair. "I ..." he stammered. "I mean, well, Liz ..."

"Now," she said.

He got to his feet, not sure of himself, gazing at her with consternation, wondering if she meant it or was joking or was drunk. "Hell, Liz, I just don't—"

"You don't want to?"

He came to the sofa and dropped next to her. He looked into her face without speaking. His hands came up and he touched his fingers to her face. He leaned over her. She closed her eyes, offering her lips to him, and he brought his mouth down on hers, lightly at first, just brushing her lips. She opened her mouth. He kissed her hard. She dug her nails into his back and pulled him against her.

When they parted she was breathing heavily. She opened her eyes slowly. Nothing had changed. He was still Hugh and she was still herself and they were holding on to one another and there was the same bliss.

"I love you, Liz."

"Yes." She pulled him to her. "Yes."

"I never stopped."

"I thought about you," she whispered. "I never stopped thinking about you."

"I've found you again. I want to keep you. I don't want to let you go again."

"Just hold me. Kiss me."

He kissed her again. Her heart pounded and her skin was burning. His hand moved along her arm and shoulder, along her back. His finger brushed lightly over her breast and she shuddered with pleasure. She pressed against him, her senses reeling.

"I want you, Liz."

Like before. Wipe away the years. Wipe away the unhappiness. Wipe away everything. "Yes," she said, "yes."

His hand caressed her. His lips touched her eyes, settled over her ear. She squirmed against him. "Not here," she said.

He released her, got up and pulled her to her feet. She leaned against him. He swung her into his arms and carried her to the stairs, then up, slowly, a step at a time. Her face was nuzzled into his neck and she felt peaceful and wanted and protected.

Moving along the hall, he peered into the bedrooms, found hers, knowing it because it was the largest. He carried her to the bed and put her down carefully. He pulled her shoes off, then reached to unzipper her dress.

"I'll do it," she said. "Your hands are shaking." She got to her feet and undressed.

He was waiting for her by the side of the bed. She dropped the last of her clothing and went to him, curling her arms about him, pressing herself close to him, leaning her cheek against the hair on his chest.

"Mother!" a shrill voice screamed from the doorway.

Elizabeth snapped erect and spun away, stunned by the shock in the voice. She faced the horrified expression of Debbie. Stepping back, she cowered and tried to cover her nakedness with her hands. She fought for something to say, some way to explain, anything to take away the growing look of hatred on her daughter's face. "I didn't hear you come in," she said.

"That, I'd say, is pretty damned obvious!"

Elizabeth began to shake. The sudden shock and shame on top of a nervous system brought to fever pitch by a mounting passion, coupled with the dulling effects of the liquor, erupted into sudden hysteria. Elizabeth buried her face in her hands and began to laugh.

"Mother!" Debbie screamed. "How can you laugh?!"

Elizabeth fell back against a table. The laughter shook her body, rose in frenzied peals. Her face was contorted with the mirthless, wracking laugh and tears ran down her face.

Frozen into immobility, Hugh came to his senses. "She's hysterical," he snapped. He reached out and grasped Elizabeth's shoulders and shook her. He slapped her face and the laughter stopped as suddenly as it had begun.

"Oh!" Debbie cried. She turned away from the doorway and ran, the sobs of anguish and anger trailing her.

"Debbie!" Elizabeth screamed. She tore loose from Hugh's grasp and ran to the doorway and into the hall. "Debbie!"

The front door slammed. Elizabeth sagged against the railing over the stairs. She began to cry and dropped to her knees in the carpeted hall. Hugh knelt beside her and held her shoulders.

"She's gone!" Elizabeth wailed. "She's gone!"

"She'll be back," Hugh said, trying to gentle her.

"What have I done, Hugh? What have I done? My own daughter to see me like that! Oh, my God, it's horrible! I've lost her, Hugh, I've lost her!"

"You can never lose a daughter," Hugh said.

"But I have! How can I ever face her again? What could I ever say to her?"

"I don't know, Elizabeth."

She leaned against him and cried until there were no more tears. Then she got to her feet. She turned and walked back to the bedroom and picked up her clothes. She dropped into a chair, her shoulders slumped with weariness. "I suppose she'll call Brad," she said. "Well, it had to happen sooner or later. First it was Chet Parker—"

"Don't, Liz."

"—then you, then it would be someone else."

"You know that's not true," Hugh said.

Elizabeth buried her face in her hands, then she lifted her face and she felt a numbness. "My life as I know it has ended," she said. "Just like that. And I'm sorry. I'm truly sorry."

"I'll make you a new life, Liz."

She shook her head. "No," she said, "however it works out, I'll have to try to pick up the pieces of this one. I felt young again with you, but that's just my age, I suppose. I'm thirty-six, and my mind fights against it. For a moment I thought I could be eighteen again. But we can't. We have to be what we are. I've never had to beg before, but I'm going to beg them to forgive me. I know they never will, and I know I'll suffer, but I have to try."

Hugh stared at her for a long moment, then he began to dress. "We had better find her," he said. "I think she'll need someone."

Mike Roberts paced the thick carpet of the bedroom with the restless fury of a caged animal. The hour since dinner had only served to heighten his anger.

"Dirt," he said over and over again. "They got the damn nerve to call me dirt!"

His hands were balled into tight fists and buried in the pockets of the silk robe. Back and forth, back and forth he paced. The muscles in his neck bulged and his anger was like a tight ball in his chest.

It's that kid, that damn snooty kid. Figures I ain't good enough for her. Not good enough. There ain't the woman been born that I can't make crawl. They're all the same, every damned one of them.

Claire hadn't said a word after he hit her and she was still downstairs. The other bitch was locked in her room. He knew her kind. Tease you and then lock the door. Yeah, he knew that kind all right. She'd find out. She'd damn soon find out!

He went to the door and jerked it open. He strode along the hall until he reached Beverly's room. He gripped the door knob and shook it. "Open this door!" There was no answer from within. "You hear me? I said to open this goddamn door!" Still no answer. He turned away and went to the head of the stairs. "Claire," he shouted.

Claire came to the base of the stairs. "What do you want?" she asked.

"Come up here!"

"No."

"You just better get up here, Baby, because that fancy kid of yours is gonna get it."

"You leave her alone!"

"I told you, didn't I? I told you?"

"Don't you lay a finger on her!"

"I'm having her, see!"

"Don't touch her!"

"You coming up here? You gonna watch?"

"I'm calling the police!"

"Call 'em! Call the goddamn Marines! Call the National Guard! You're gonna need them!" He swung away from the stairs.

"No!" Claire screamed. "No!" She turned from the stairs and ran to the kitchen.

Mike went to Beverly's door. He felt exhilarated. He hammered on the panels with his fists. "Open up!" He jigged back to the far wall, bent and hunched his shoulders. He flung himself forward and hit the door. The hinges groaned. He danced back, then drove forward again. He was laughing. He fell back against the wall, then threw himself into the door. The top hinge tore out of the woodwork and the door canted. He danced back, then drove forward, toppling the door and bursting into the room.

Beverly was crouched against the far wall. She held a letter opener out before her. "Don't come near me!"

Mike laughed. He stripped the bathrobe off his shoulders and paraded naked, making a half-circle around her. "Like what you see? All muscle, Baby, and all yours."

"Stay away from me. I warn you, I'll use this!"

"You got it all wrong, Honey. I ain't the one's gonna get stabbed." He grinned and came towards her, crouched, wary, his eyes on the letter opener. "I'm gonna take that away from you, and you're gonna be glad I did. This is gonna be a big night for you, Kid." He was a foot away from her outstretched hand. He feinted to the left and she stabbed at his arm. His right hand whipped up and closed over her wrist. She screamed as he jerked her forward. The letter opener clattered to the floor. She swept her nails out to claw him, but he grasped her wrist and spun her around. He grabbed her robe and jerked her to her knees in the process of tearing it from her.

"No!" she screamed. "No! No!"

He swung the back of his hand and cracked her across the mouth. She gasped in terror. He reached down and tore away the buttons of her pajama blouse. He closed his hands over her breasts and pulled her to her feet, laughing at her cry of sudden pain. He flung her back onto the bed.

Beverly's hands flew up instinctively to cover her breasts. Mike grabbed the legs of the pajama trousers and jerked them down over her hips. Beverly kicked, screaming, fought him with her fists, but he stripped them from her legs and flung them aside.

"Now, Baby!"

Claire burst into the room. "Mike! Stop it! You're mad!"

"Wanna watch, huh? Okay, just stand aside!"

Beverly tried to crab away from him, but he grasped her ankles and dragged her back. She sat up to fight him off, but he slapped her hard across the face, stifling her scream.

"Leave her alone, Mike!" Claire screamed.

Mike pushed Beverly's shoulders back to the bed. She clawed her nails over his chest, leaving angry red lines. She crossed her legs, locked her ankles. He kneeled over her.

"Mike! Get off her!" Claire shouted.

Beverly raked her nails over his eyes and he bellowed with pain. He tried to force his knee between her legs, and she strained against him. He doubled his fist and punched her in the stomach. She gagged and her legs relaxed.

"I swear, Mike, get off her!"

"Shut up!"

He pressed down against her, butting her with his knees. She whimpered and shook her head from side to side as her strength left her.

Claire ran to the bed and stood behind him. "Mike, stop!"

"No, damn you!"

Beverly screamed and her body recoiled and arched with pain as he forced himself toward his goal.

Claire's face was twisted with torment. A sob strangled in her throat. Her arm swept over her head. The long blade of the butcher knife glittered for a second in the light before she plunged it into his back.

He expelled the air from his lungs in a single gasp. He was dead the instant the knife entered his heart, but his body jerked with nerve spasms. Beverly's eyes were wide with shock and horror.

Claire had dropped to her knees. She was sobbing. "Mike, I told you not to. I couldn't let you."

Beverly touched the lifeless shoulders. She twisted and cast the body away from her. She slithered from the bed, backed away until she reached the doorway. The shock was still great upon her and she trembled, unable to make a sound. She saw the blood beginning to spread, saw the handle of the knife protruding from his back. She clasped a hand to her mouth and ran from the room. She flew down the stairs and grabbed the telephone. She dialed the number automatically.

When the telephone rang Cora Masserly knitted her brow with annoyance, thinking that it was Marcia calling back. She went to the hall and lifted the receiver, her mind forming the words of refusal.

"Hello," she said.

"Let me talk to Sam," the female voice said. It was a voice edged with panic.

"Who is this?" Cora asked.

"Let me talk to Sam," the voice insisted, then added with emphasis, "Please!"

"I'm afraid I'll have to know who is speaking," Cora said, the frown deep on her face. The woman on the line was crying and it baffled her.

"What is it?" Sam asked from the living room.

"I'll handle it," Cora said.

"I must talk to Sam," the voice shrilled.

"What nonsense is this?" Cora asked. A knot of fear was growing within her, born of the urgency in the voice. What could Sam possibly have to do with—.

"Who is it?" Sam asked, coming into the hall.

"Some female," Cora said. "I think she's drunk."

"Give me it," Sam said.

"I'll handle it," Cora said.

Sam reached out and wrenched the receiver from her grasp. "Sam!" she said. Sam ignored her and Cora caught her breath. He turned his back on her and said into the phone, "Hello, this is Sam."

"Sam!" Beverly cried. "Oh, Sam, I need you!"

"What's the trouble?"

"Sam, come here right away! I need you! Now!"

"All right," he said, "but tell me what's wrong." He felt his pulse begin to throb.

"It's Mike," she said. "He's … he's dead!"

"What?"

"He's dead!" She began to cry. "Mother killed him," she wailed. "Oh, Sam, please! I need you!"

"What happened?"

"I can't talk about it! He tried to rape me! It was horrible, I don't—"

"I'll be right there!" Sam said. He dropped the phone in the cradle and started for the door.

"Sam!" Cora barked. "Where are you going?"

"Out. I have to go out."

"What do you mean, out? Who was that woman?"

"Beverly Merrick," Sam said, his hand on the door knob. "She's in trouble."

"Why would she call you?"

"I can't talk about it now," Sam said.

"This is preposterous, Sam! You can't run out into the night for some stranger! I forbid it!"

"You forbid it?"

"Yes! I'm your wife!"

"Cora," Sam said, "let's get one thing straight. You've never been my wife. You've been my advisor, my guiding light, but you've never been a wife."

"Sam, if you go out of this house, don't come back!"

"Cora, stop threatening me. I have no intention of coming back to this house, this palace of frigidity. I'm in love with this girl. Does that surprise you? Does that dirty word shock you? Love! It's a four-letter word, Cora, and you don't like four-letter words. Well, they exist, whether you like them or not. Love, Cora, think about it sometime. Something you've never known. It hasn't anything to do with Masters Degrees or social position or letting someone have sex with you to get what you want. But it's real, Cora, and I love this girl, and that's where I'm going!" He jerked the door open.

"Sam!" Cora screamed. "Don't go!"

The door slammed and she heard the sound of his footsteps running down the walk.

CHAPTER FOURTEEN

So that's what I get for five years of waiting on him, Cora thought. I might have known it. They're all alike. I give him five years of my life and he runs to the first little harlot who waggles her finger.

Cora had stood by the window, her hands shaking with anger. Then she had wandered through the house, denouncing him. She went to the kitchen and mixed a drink. An hour and four drinks had passed and her ashtray was littered with cigarette butts, crushed and twisted stumps of unabated frustration.

He'll pay for this, she said to herself. He'll come crawling back here, begging me to take him back, and he'll pay dearly for what he said. I know him, he's weak, he'll be back.

She sat quietly, listening to the sounds of the house in the stillness. She got up and paced nervously, then went back to the kitchen to mix another drink. She glanced at the clock and it was almost nine. She stopped pouring and put the bottle down. She gulped what she had in the glass, then turned abruptly and went through the living room and into the hall.

Her nerves were on edge. I can't stand being in this house alone, she thought. Not tonight, not after what he said. Men are beasts, damned ungrateful beasts. She picked the telephone receiver up and dialed.

"Hello," she said, "Marcia?"

"Cora," Marcia said. "You've changed your mind."

"Yes. Is that party still on?"

"I'll say it is," Marcia said. "I was just about to leave. I'll be by in five minutes."

"I'll be ready," Cora said. She put the receiver down. I'll show him, she thought. I'm not going to sit around here while he goes chasing his trollops. She hurried up the stairs to change her dress.

Sylvia Thompson sat at the bar in the Ferry Inn. She was nursing her scotch and soda.

Don't want to be drunk, she thought. Want to know what's going on.

She had sat in her parked car watching his window when she had first arrived at the Inn, sat there smoking for a half hour. When the light went out she had come into the bar. This was her second drink. She had been in the bar for a half hour.

This has to be done just right, she thought, just right. Her mounting excitement made her fidgety. This will be like winning the Grand National, she thought. They ought to have a trophy for this one. She chuckled. That's what I need, a damn trophy room. Subconsciously, Sylvia sought the Holy Grail of sex, the conquering of the urge. She sought the hated father image, her tormented psyche believing that through seduction and subsequent shaming of the image she would be released from the obsessive demands of the libido.

She twisted her glass, making rings on the bar. She glanced about her. A couple sat at one of the tables, their heads together in smiling conversation. A single man sat at the end of the bar and kept his eyes on her chest. The door to the garden was open and there was the drone of conversation from a large dinner party. This was punctuated by the meaningless, sporadic chortles of laughter from a drunk who sat alone at a table near the stone wall.

Sylvia slipped from the stool and left the bar. She went up the stairway to the second floor, then along the hallway, the carpet muffling her steps. She stopped by his door and listened. From within came the sound of snoring. She smiled and her hand rested on the door knob. There were no locks on the doors at the Ferry Inn. She turned the knob carefully, nudged the door with her shoulder. A hinge creaked, but she slipped inside and closed it quietly. She stood by the door letting her eyes become accustomed to the semi-darkness. The diffused light from a street lamp filtered into the room.

Moving to the foot of the bed, she stared at the mound of covers. She slipped off her shoes, then padded to the side of the bed and began to unbutton her blouse. She dropped each garment onto a nearby chair. Finally she stood nude in the half-light, trembling with excitement, anticipating his reaction. She leaned over, took the edge of the covers in her fingers and pulled them down slowly.

The bedsprings creaked with the addition of her weight. She slid her legs down, careful not to touch him, then she moved up to his back and wrapped her left arm about him.

Ira Wilson came awake with a start. He was confused for a moment, then, realizing that someone was in the bed with him, he cried out with alarm and leaped from the bed. He fell against the wall, groping for the light switch, assailed with terror. He found the switch and flooded the room with light.

Sylvia was kneeling in the middle of the bed and her arms were outstretched to him. "Come back," she said.

"What do you want?" His eyes bugged at her nakedness, at the voluptuousness of her body. He pressed back against the wall, as though trying to get farther away from the vision.

Sylvia read the fright in his eyes. She had to resist the impulse to laugh. He wore an old-fashioned night shirt of striped cotton and his appearance was comical. "Come back to bed," she said, tilting her head to the side and smiling. "I want you."

"Get out of here!" His voice was a strangled whisper.

"I have to have you," Sylvia said.

"Whore!" he said, spitting the word, as though it was too distasteful to speak.

"No," Sylvia said. "I'm your lover. Come." She began to edge off the bed.

"Filth!" Wilson rasped. "Filth!"

Sylvia came off the bed and advanced slowly, her hands out to him, moving with seductive precision. Wilson's hands came up to ward her off. A tick started in his right cheek. Sylvia stopped before him.

Wilson's teeth chattered and nausea gripped his stomach. It was coming over him again, the burning hatred. His mind was revolving back in time to the week-end with Uncle Arthur when he, Ira, was fifteen and Uncle Arthur said that he should be a man, and Uncle Arthur's friend, the woman with orange hair named Sarah. The memory made him shake. Uncle Arthur making him undress and the woman with the red laughing mouth standing in front of him compounding his shame with her nakedness, her breasts shaking, and her laugh making the mound of her stomach tremble, and Uncle Arthur behind her, laughing, urging him on, and the woman enveloping him, clutching his head and pressing his face into the sweat-perfume of her until he screamed and beat at her with his fists and the woman shouted, 'Crazy little bastard,' and Uncle Arthur pulled him off her, and then he had vomited, and Uncle Arthur had knocked him to the floor.

It came over him now, the panorama of never-forgotten horror, and before him, twisting and smiling, was the incarnation of wanton evil, the symbol of woman's innate depravity. Her features were blurred by his mounting fury, but he saw the form of her, saw the evil gestures.

Wilson lunged away from the wall and fell upon her with the wrath of an avenging angel. He pummelled her with his fists. Sylvia cried out, but more in pleasure than in pain, and threw herself against his chest. Her hands gripped the nightshirt. Wilson flung her from him and the shirt tore down the front. Sylvia grabbed his legs, tripping him, and they rolled on the floor together. She crawled onto his back and he threw her off, but she carried away the rest of the shirt. He sprung to his feet, naked now, his face twisted with anger.

"Filth!" he shouted. "Vile, dirty thing!" He kicked at her and she sprawled, but she came to her feet quickly and rushed at him, her arms flailing. He swung his fist, hitting her in the face, and she staggered back to the bed. He fell upon her, beating her, cursing with each blow. She twisted from the bed and gripped his thighs with her arms. He pulled away, dragging her with him, beating upon her back and shoulders with his fists. He kicked her away from him and reeled across the room, staggering drunkenly, waving his fists, bellowing curses.

Sylvia could not get up. Her mouth was split and bleeding, and her front teeth were broken. One eye was swollen closed and the pain shot through her head. She laughed, gagging on blood. She was being punished for her sins, the punishment she wanted. She dragged herself to her feet, saw Wilson through one eye. She knew that she had to finish it. She went after him.

Wilson's tortured mind was teetering on the edge of sanity. His heart pounded and his breath came in gasps. He saw her approach. A savage cry gurgled in his throat. He leaped at her, smashing her down. Wild laughter burst from his mouth, and he ran to the door and wrenched it open.

There were people in the hallway, a small knot of terrified and curious faces gathered around the doorway, attracted by the sounds of violence within. They fell back as Wilson rushed from the room, startled by his sudden appearance and the onslaught of maniacal laughter. He rushed past them and down the hall.

"He's nuts!" A man exclaimed.

"He's going downstairs naked as a jaybird!"

They watched Wilson's flight, then turned and pressed against the open doorway, eager to view the carnage. A woman gasped and one of the men whistled through his teeth.

"It's that Thompson woman."

"Beat the hell out of her."

"My God, would you look at that. What a pair on her!"

"A real looney!"

Wilson rushed down the stairs as though pursued by the Devil. He burst into the bar. A woman screamed. He stopped and shook his fist at her. "Filth!" he shouted. He bounded across the room, leaving the bartender with his mouth agape, and ran out into the garden. He leaped onto a table next to the large dinner party and pointed his finger at one of the women. "Harlot!" he screamed. "You're all alike! Harlots!"

The drunk at the table by the wall straightened in his chair and blinked. "You tell 'em, Buddy," he shouted, clapping his hands.

The woman screamed at the sight of the naked wraith on the table and buried her face in her hands. The men kept to their chairs, too startled to move.

"Vessels of evil!" Wilson shouted, shaking his finger. "Hoydens of perverted lust!"

"You tell 'em, Buddy!" the drunk shouted.

"Bitches! The wrath of God will descend upon you for your wickedness!"

"Give 'em Hell, pal," the drunk shouted, gleefully leaping up and down in his chair.

"The evil in your bodies will be purged by the fires of everlasting—"

The bartender ended the sermon with a flying tackle that sent Wilson tumbling into the bushes, bellowing with rage. The two men wrestled, the bartender finally twisting Wilson's arm behind his back. Two men from the dinner party helped to hold him down.

"Somebody call the cops," the bartender said. "This baby needs a strait jacket."

Sam Masserly skidded to a stop before the house. He ran up to the front door and turned the knob, entering the house unannounced.

The living room was empty. "Beverly," he called, advancing into the room. There was no answer. "Beverly," he called again, baffled by the silence. He went to the stairway and stopped. Dr. Willard Curran was coming down the stairs.

"Hello, Sam," Curran said.

"Where is she?"

"I got her to sleep," the doctor said. He reached the bottom of the stairs and stopped.

"What happened?"

"Sit down over here and I'll tell you as much as I know." He went into the living room and Sam followed.

"Is Beverly all right?"

Doctor Curran shrugged. "I don't know," he said. "I administer drugs, set bones. Physically, she's fine."

"On the phone she said—"

"She was raped," Doctor Curran said. "But it won't kill her. Sit down."

Sam sat on the edge of a chair and faced the doctor. His hands were clenched. "How about Roberts?"

"He's dead. Died instantly. Claire stabbed him in the back while he was still on top of the girl."

Sam grimaced. "That's murder."

"Homicide," the doctor said. "I imagine the coroner's jury will pronounce it justifiable. That remains to be seen."

"And Beverly—"

"She's still in a state of shock, but she's fine as far as I can tell. Tomorrow it may be different. She called me, and she told me that she had called you. I had to insist that she take the sedative because she was waiting for you. I take it that you're involved with the girl."

Sam wasn't prepared for the statement and the word 'involved' made it sound illicit. He nodded his head.

"Seriously?" the doctor asked.

"Yes."

"Your wife know about it?"

"Look, Doctor, I don't see that this is any of your—"

"It is my business, Sam, because now that girl is my patient, and I want to know anything that might have an effect on her recovery."

"I'm in love with her," Sam said. "Cora knows it. I'm going to get a divorce."

"The fact that Beverly was attacked isn't going to change your mind?"

"Certainly not!" Sam snapped angrily. "Why should it?"

"I only asked. But it might make a difference. Rape is a strange crime, Sam. In actuality it is only a case of forced copulation, something that happens to millions of women every night, and the victim is seldom injured physically. What it does mentally is a different story. Sex to a young girl is generally associated with love. She sees herself giving herself to a gentle, desiring lover. She sees it as the union conceived in loving. It has a poetic quality, a beauty. With this picture in mind, if she is forced through brutal lust her femininity is shamed and she is repelled by the act. It suddenly takes on only the vilest aspects. It is a shock to the mind more than the body or the nervous system.

"Is Beverly—?"

"Beverly is still in shock, but I can say this for certain, she is going to need patience and understanding and a lot of tenderness. You'll have to realize what she's been through. It will take time before she can ever make love with a man and not bring back a memory of horror. And you'll also have to understand that a man was murdered on top of her. Are you sure that you're big enough to undertake this?"

"I don't know," Sam said. "I know I want to try."

The doctor smiled. "That's all any of us can do, Sam. I have a feeling that it will be worth the effort."

A car pulled into the drive and stopped.

"That will be the Township police," the doctor said. "I called them."

"Will they arrest Claire?"

"As a formality, yes. But they can't take her tonight. I put her under sedation, too."

"Is it okay if I stay here? I'd like to see Beverly when she comes around."

"That will be good." He went to the door to admit the policemen.

Hugh was driving. Sitting beside him, Elizabeth Pennington was thinking about God. They had been to the homes of two of Debbie's friends and were now on the way to a third. The Township Police Car had passed them on Bradley Road and its red lights had been blinking and she had wondered where it was going, and who could possibly have more trouble on this night than she did. And then she thought about Debbie and the police car and her heartbeat had quickened, but no, Debbie was not that foolish. And now she was thinking of God.

He makes us the way we are, she thought. He gives us all the desires that must be satisfied and it is always the desires that destroy us. If Greed, for instance, is evil, why didn't He just create us without it? It only took Him six days to create the world, she said to herself, but He might have done a damned sight better job if He had taken more time. Pretty haphazard job if you ask me. It's almost as if He has a great diabolical sense of humor, as if he created man for His amusement, filled us with urges and needs and moral codes, and just watches to see us fall on our collective faces. Brother, I'll bet He's getting a chuckle out of the mess I've made. And why is God always *He*? Why masculine? Well, why not, He's God isn't He? Capital *He*, a man's God, the man's world. If Brad wants a woman and tumbles some New York floozy, so what? I'm supposed to shrug and say, "Well, that's the way it is. A man will always be off slaying dragons. That's their nature."

But just let *me* do it and I'm a leper because I'm a woman. And all because God is a He. Could this be the reason that most of the church-goers are women? Is it possible that they're really in there worshipping Men, not necessarily Him, but the whole concept of Male? Who knows, she mused, who knows?

They were approaching the Blakely house. "It's the first drive on your right," she said and Hugh nodded. What will I say to her? What can I say?

Hugh turned the car into the drive and stopped. "Want me to ask? The car isn't here."

"No," Elizabeth said wearily, "I'll ask." She got out of the car and walked to the front door. It was already being opened by Susan Blakely. "Hello, Susan," Elizabeth said. "I was wondering if Debbie had been here."

The girl gripped the door and her eyes were wide. "She was, Mrs. Pennington, but she's gone."

"Oh." Elizabeth felt the relief of not having to face her daughter in front of strangers. "Did she go home?"

The girl shook her head. "She came to use the phone. She called her father in New York. She ... she was crying ... and ... well, she went to Trenton to take the train."

"I see," Elizabeth said, trying to keep the despair out of her voice. By the girl's expression she knew that Debbie had been explicit in the phone conversation to Brad. "Well, thank you." She walked back to the car and got in.

"Was she here?" Hugh asked.

"Yes."

"She go home?"

"Yes, she went home," Elizabeth said, then added, "to her Father."

Hugh said nothing as he started the car and drove away. Elizabeth spoke only to give directions. Finally Hugh said, "I'm sorry, Liz."

"It's over with," she said.

"Nothing ends, Liz," Hugh said. "A life that nourishes on another life is part of that life."

"The intellectual approach won't help, Hugh. I've lost my baby, and that's a fact!"

"She's a grown girl with a mind and will of her own," Hugh said. "She grew within you and was yours, but the moment she was ready to come into her own life, she was no longer yours, you had no recourse but to let her come down through your body and be herself. You were there to care for her, but already her will was being formed. You were given her care and only ego makes you believe that she was yours, that you possessed her!" Hugh took a deep breath. "And in the same way that you do not own her, she does not own you! And if she will forsake you for loving when she knows the circumstances, then she's not worth bothering about! Damn it, Liz, I love you! I'm glad of what has happened because I want to marry you!"

Elizabeth stared at Hugh. It was the first time he had ever spoken sharply to her. She saw him with an added dimension. He was no longer just Good Hugh, Gentle, Wise Hugh—he had a stern, forceful side on which a woman could lean. She liked this.

Hugh turned the car into her drive and parked. "Want me to come in?"

Elizabeth shook her head. "Not tonight, Hugh," she said. "I think I want to be by myself. I want to think."

"Think about what I said."

"I will." She got out of the car. "Will you call me tomorrow?"

"First thing in the morning. I love you, Liz."

"Thank you, Hugh," she said. "I think I need that." She closed the door and walked to the house.

Cora was too drunk to think clearly, and she did not know what she was doing in the bedroom, or why Marcia was fighting with the big woman named Clara. She was on the large bed and her head was spinning, Marcia said. "I brought her here!"

Yes, she thought, Marcia brought me. I wanted to get away from the house, away from the things Sam said. Just wanted to get drunk, forget everything, called Marcia.

She had known immediately upon entering the house that it was a strange party. Her first reaction had been one of panic. She had heard about the parties on Temperance Hill, not really believing the stories of wild orgies, thinking that nothing like that could really go on just a mile above a town like Walkers Ferry. Her next reaction while she was being guided into the room by Marcia had been curiosity.

There were about two-dozen women in the room, many of them dressed like men. Cora recognized several of the guests, having seen them on the street, but the rest were strangers. It took her several minutes to realize that the women were paired into couples, and she stared in confusion at a square-shouldered woman kissing a pretty blonde girl.

Marcia pressed a drink into her hand. "Surprised?" Marcia asked.

"A ... a little," Cora said. Nervously, she gulped the drink, asked for another. Marcia laughed and pointed to the stairway. Cora looked and caught her breath. A nude woman was coming down the stairs. She was big, with a square face and short brown hair swept back over her ears. She could have been a man except for the large breasts that flopped with each step. There was a crudity about her, and the way she managed to mimic a man was grotesque and horrifying to Cora.

"That's Clara," Marcia said. "This is her house. She's a real card, you'll have to meet her."

And now, lying on the bed, unable to collect her thoughts, Cora heard Clara snarl, "That's just tough. You brought her and I got her. This is *my* house, see, *my* house, and in *my* house I damn well do what I want."

Marcia protested, but Clara forced her out of the room and slammed the door. Cora giggled. They were fighting over her

and it was funny because she wasn't a lesbian. She wanted to tell
Clara, but the words would not form. Drunk, she said to herself, too drunk. Clara settled on the bed beside her and began
to stroke her with her hands. Then Clara was kissing her and
she wanted to laugh and tell Clara that she had made a mistake,
but she was going to sleep. Yes, go to sleep and then Clara would
take her hands away. She felt her dress being unbuttoned as she
slipped into darkness, a deep, drugged sleep.

The door slammed open and she came awake. She was sober,
and her mouth felt thick and she was sick at the stomach and her
head ached. There was shouting and she shook her head. She sat
erect in the bed. Clara was standing and Marcia was framed in
the doorway.

"Come and look at it!" Marcia screamed. "Come and look at
your goddamned house!"

Female screams, high and shrill and filled with panic, came
from the floor below.

"It's on fire!" Marcia shouted. "And I hope that the goddamned thing burns to the ground, and I hope you burn with it,
you damned bull dyke!"

Cora scrambled from the bed. Clara bellowed with rage and
rushed from the room in pursuit of Marcia. Cora found that she
was only half-dressed. She could see the flickering shadows of
flames. Marcia had said the house was on fire. She could not find
her shoes. She fumbled with the buttons of her dress, gave it up.
She looked for her purse, found it on the bedside table. She ran
from the room and into the hall. From the top of the stairs she
could see the fire raging in the kitchen and spreading into the
living room. She ran down the stairs. The front door was open
and she rushed out into the night.

The women stood on the lawn and in the driveway, some
danced about in confusion. One girl was wrapped in a blanket,
another was clothed only in a pair of brief panties.

"Call the fire department!" Clara bellowed.

"I did," someone said. "Listen, you can hear the siren."

Cora ran across the lawn. She had to get away, she couldn't be there when the firemen arrived. What would the town say? Her, a respectable woman, at a party on Temperance Hill! She started up the drive, the small stones cutting her feet. She heard Marcia call to her. She ran faster. Not the road, no, not that way! They would come up the road. She veered off across the lawn, stumbled and fell. She dropped her purse and started to grope for it, then she heard Marcia coming after her. She lurched to her feet and ran, crashing through the brush. She had to get away! Had to! She fell down a small bank, got to her feet and ran. Briars tore at her arms and hands. Her body ached and her breath came in tight, strangling gasps. She plunged through the dense brush in the dark, falling and stumbling, picking herself up and running, pushed on by her panic, the terrible fear that brought wracking sobs from her throat.

She stopped to catch her breath. Turning, she saw the flames rising against the dark sky, a billowing pillar of red. She heard the approaching siren. Her fear grew anew. She turned and ran again. Get away! Get away!

CHAPTER FIFTEEN

Athena sat close to David with her head on his shoulder. He drove with both hands on the wheel, turning his face at intervals to kiss her forehead.

"I feel swept off my feet," Athena said.

"That's how we Belsons always get our women," David said.

"You mean you don't club them and drag them away?"

"Grandfather did that. Nowadays we sweep them."

Athena laughed lightly. "David?"

"What?"

"I'm happy. I'm very happy."

"I'm glad," he said.

They drove in silence for a time, then Athena said, "David, when are you going to make an honorable woman of me?"

"We'll get the license tomorrow."

"Hmmmm, good. I think I'm going to like keeping house for you."

The headlights probed the darkness of the road before them, outlined something moving in the near distance. David leaned forward and blinked, easing off on the gas pedal. "What's that?"

Athena sat up and looked. "It's someone walking in the road," she said.

"He looks drunk," David said.

He slowed the car. The headlights picked up and held the figure that staggered in the middle of the road, the arms flailing for balance. The car drew closer.

"It's a woman!" Athena said.

The figure staggered and fell. David pulled up and stopped. He leaped from the car. Athena was getting out the other side. David ran to the crumpled figure in the road. It was a woman. Her legs and arms were cut and scratched. Her dress was torn and covered with mud. Her hair was a mess of tangles and briars. He turned her over and her face was a cross-hatch of cuts and bruises. He began to lift her, and she suddenly came to life. He saw terror leap into her eyes. She snarled, the broken lips curling back over small white teeth. She squirmed, kicking, and lashed out at him with her nails.

Taken by surprise, David released her and stepped back. The woman whirled and ran across the road.

"Hey, wait a minute," David said. "Wait. We'll help you!"

The woman plunged off the road and ran down the embankment and into the thick brush and darkness. The sounds of her flight were evident for several minutes, then there was silence.

"Who was it?" Athena asked. "Why did she run?"

"I don't know," David said. "She suddenly looked at me, and was frightened and fought to get away. She was like an animal. I had the feeling I had seen her before."

"Wonder what happened?" Athena said.

"I guess there's no point trying to find her," David said. "She obviously doesn't want to be helped."

"Running around out here in the dark," Athena said. "Brrr, it gives me the willies. Maybe she was someone's date and decided it would be better to get out and walk."

"She was all scratched up," David said.

"I'm glad I have an honorable man," Athena said. "Come along, honorable man, I'm beginning to feel the call of home and hearth."

David wrapped his arm about her and they went back to the car. When she got in he closed the door and went to the driver's side, casting a glance into the darkness at the side of the road. He got behind the wheel and drove off.

Crouched in the brush, Cora waited until she saw the car drive away. She smiled with appreciation of her own cunning. Can't take the chance of anyone seeing me like this. When I get home it will be fine. She got to her feet and climbed back to the road. She walked along slowly, letting her strength gather. Her feet hurt and her body was a mass of burns from the cuts. She saw the lights of another car approaching and she scurried off the road and hid in the bushes until it went past.

She got up again and walked. It was all his fault, all Sam's. He would pay for this! When she got home and there would be no way of anyone knowing, then he'd pay.

The fire was extinguished and the firemen were gathering up their equipment. There were three trucks and a number of cars. It was a volunteer fire company and the firemen were the townsmen of Walkers Ferry, mostly the sons and grandsons of the more permanent residents, the unsophisticated portion of the town.

"Queer party," one of them mumbled. "All women. Damndest thing."

"How did it start?"

"One of them got jealous because her girlfriend was with another woman."

"Jesus."

"Crazy damn thing."

"She poured kerosene all over the kitchen and put a match to it."

"She did a good job. That joint ain't worth ten cents now."

"I can't understand that kind of thing with women."

"You see them two blondes? God, they're nice stuff."

"Damn waste of female, you ask me."

A young fireman wearing a pair of rubber boots folded to his knees came up to the first truck where the Chief was talking with the men and directing the reassemblage of equipment. He held a woman's purse in his hand. "I found this in the grass over there," he said.

The Chief took the purse in his hands, turned it over, pursing his lips. "Guess it belongs to one of them," he said. "It ought to have a name in it."

He opened it and held it to the light and peered inside. He reached his hand in and brought out a wallet. Opening the wallet, he extracted a driver's license and read the name. "I'll be damned," he said. He handed the license to one of the men. "Look at that."

"Cora Masserly," the man said. "Well, I'll be go to hell. Imagine that. I never figured her to be one of them."

CHAPTER SIXTEEN

Howard Denby, public relations man, angled across Sixth Avenue in New York City, cutting a straight and true course for Moriarity's Steak House.

It was after the lunch hour, but he did not have food on his mind. He was preoccupied with his recent state of unemployment.

He paused at the entrance to Moriarity's, gripped the door handle and pulled it open. He went in, nodded at the headwaiter, and went to the long bar. He saw people he knew. There were several public relations men at the bar, a press agent for a Broadway show, a famous columnist, and a clutch of freelance writers for the bigger magazines.

Howard Denby took a stool and ordered his usual scotch on the rocks.

"Hear your boss went off his chump," the press agent said. "Tough luck."

"That's the way it crumbles," Howard said. He knew that everyone had heard about Ira Wilson. It was perfect tabloid material and the *Daily News* had two-decked the front page banner: *Sexologist Runs Amok!*

"It's a lousy life," one of the public relations men said. "You figure you've got the golden egg and zippo, it goes through your fingers."

"The secret," Howard said bitterly, "is to make sure that your golden egg don't get laid."

The men laughed and Howard felt better. It was a good line and he'd be quoted at Sardis and some of the better joints. A little talk around might bring up a good client.

"What you got cooking?" one of them asked.

"A few irons in the fire," Howard said.

One of the magazine writers came down the bar and took the stool next to Howard. "You were close to Wilson," he said. "Why don't you write a book about the survey business."

"*Argus Magazine* owns all the reports," Howard said.

"I mean a novel."

"Nah," Howard said. "Nothing there. Statistics, that's all. Figures. How many times you do this, how many times you do that. Just figures. It looks jazzy in the magazine article, but in a book you gotta have people. Conflict, man, ya need conflict. A bunch of scientists talking to women, that ain't nothing. It's all statistics."

"I don't know," the magazine writer said. "I'm sure there's a story there somewhere."

"Look, Pal," Howard said, "take my word for it. Nothing there. Like this last time. A little jerkwater town that folds up at nine o'clock. Dullest damn place you ever saw. A parking ticket in that burg is a major event. Believe me, I was there. Genuine squaresville. Nothing could possibly happen there."

"Wilson happened there," the writer said.

Howard groaned and held his head. "Wilson ended there, and that oughta prove that nothing happens there. Wilson never touched a broad. He hits that town and it's so damn dull that even he goes off the deep end."

The writer laughed. "Maybe you're right."

"I know I'm right," Howard said. "Bartender, make that a double."

THE END